FRAT BOYS AND DORM ROOMS
Gay Erotic Stories from the Best Four Years of Your Life
Edited by Matthew Cooper

Wilton Springs Press
Wilton Manors, Florida

return to your favorite ebook retailer and purchase your own copy. Thank you for respecting the hard work of this author.

The Jock in My Dorm Room

by Matthew Cooper

It was like winning the lottery. I lucked out at the start of my junior year at State. As I was lugging the last cardboard box into my new dorm room, the Resident Assistant on my floor knocked on my open door. It was Jeremy, one of my best friends. That pretty much guaranteed me a year of not getting harassed by a fellow student whose job it would be to keep the peace and enforce the rules. But that wasn't the best thing that happened. It's what Jeremy came by to tell me.

"Hey, Daniel! You're on my floor. That's awesome," he said as he came into the room.

"Jeremy, you're my RA? That's so cool. You're not gonna be a ballbuster, are you?" I knew he wouldn't, but I felt I should ask any way.

"Dude, are you kidding me? I don't give a shit. I just needed the stipend."

"Well, that's a relief," I said.

He flopped down on the other bed in the room, which was at this point just an empty mattress. He put his hands behind his head as he lay down with one foot still on the floor, which caused his t-shirt to ride up on him a bit. I noticed the line of smooth flesh that appeared between the bottom of his shirt and his athletic shorts. Yeah, I forgot to mention—I'm gay.

When I say Jeremy is one of my close friends, well, I mean we hooked up once in freshman year. It wasn't much to talk about. We were both up in the stacks of the library, and we saw each through the books from one row to the other. He put his hand on his crotch. I did the same. He started stroking himself over his jeans. I followed his lead. He came around the shelves to stand next to me, and we jerked off together. From that day on, we were super close friends, even though we never did anything together again.

"So you're not gonna believe this," he said.

"What?"

"Your roommate. He dropped out last week. Think he transferred to another school or something. And it's way too late for them to do anything about it. So unless someone off the waiting list hasn't figured out their living situation yet, you're gonna have your own room. At least for the fall semester."

"Rob dropped out? No fucking way! Oh shit. I can't believe it. He didn't tell me."

"Believe it, dude. How awesome is that? I mean I get my own room cuz I'm the resident assistant, but now you do, too."

I immediately started rethinking my unpacking. The closets in the dorm rooms were so tiny, but now I could potentially have two. I could change without feeling weird, and not the least of my thoughts, I would be able to jerk off whenever I wanted to. Even though Rob was a nice guy, and we made great roommates, having a room to myself was golden. Thankfully it was happening so close to the start of classes, I probably didn't have to worry about getting paired up with a stranger, who could end up being an asshole or a slob, or worse, a homophobe.

Jeremy stood up and whispered to me, "We can both hook up all we want and not have to worry about a roommate barging in. That's the other reason I applied to be an RA."

I rolled my eyes and snickered, "I just wish there were more gay guys on campus."

Jeremy smiled, "Well, there are plenty of straight guys who don't mind a good blow job, trust me. And when they find out you have a room to yourself, I guarantee you'll find plenty who will knock on your door after a frat party looking for head."

"Sounds like you've had experience with that."

Jeremy just smiled and winked at me and didn't say anything more.

"So there's no chance they'll end up assigning this to someone else?"

"Well, yeah, there's always that chance. But with classes starting in a just few days, even if someone was still on a wait list, they would have made other plans by now, rented an apartment off campus or something. I think you're pretty golden." He made his way back over to my door. "And just think. Your RA will never report you."

"I should hope not," I called out to him as he walked out.

Classes started a few days later, and just as Jeremy had expected, no one was assigned to my dorm room. I started moving my stuff around and took up both closets. I wondered if I could get the university to take the second bed out of my room. I was thinking about options, like buying a cheap sofa or putting in a few chairs or a bigger table to study at.

I made a huge mistake by going to the Resident Life department and requesting that. The woman behind the desk was so snotty about it, too. "And where do you suggest we put it?"

"I mean, I don't know. I just thought no one is using it, so maybe it could be put in storage."

"All dorm rooms have two beds. That is where they belong. What room did you say you're in again?"

Fuck. "220."

She tapped on her computer a bit and then said, "Very good. I've noted the vacancy in the student housing database. If the space is needed, we'll put another student in with you."

Fuck. Why did I say anything? I should have kept it under the radar.

But despite it all, the first week of school went by, and I never heard anything about it again. I also didn't have much luck with hooking up, so I was left to jerking off constantly. At least I knew I had privacy.

I was doing really well with my classes. It was amazing how easy it was to study when you had your own room. Sometimes Jeremy would come over and hang out in my room, and we'd troll the online apps together. But either every other gay guy on campus had blocked both of us at some point in the last two years, or we were at a straight as fuck school. Even here in the all-men's dorm, which you would think any gay guys would have applied for. There wasn't even any action in the showers or bathrooms. There was no one close by on the apps. Even the library didn't seem to have any jerking or sucking going on.

The one good thing about State was that we were a powerhouse in sports. So the campus had a ton of eye candy. Gymnasts, divers, swimmers, lacrosse players, soccer. Even if I wasn't getting any, I had plenty of crushes on straight college jocks, which gave me plenty of material for the spank bank in my head.

It was about two weeks into the semester, still September, when Jeremy came knocking on my door again. It was unlocked, so he twisted the knob and came right in. "Hey D."

"Hey." I replied. He usually led with something with a bit more content than that, so I immediately got a sense of his tone. He seemed a bit morose.

"So. I got some bad news."

Fuck.

"They're putting someone in here with you."

"Fuck."

"Yeah, sorry bud. I think he's like a transfer student or something."

I couldn't think of anything else to say, so I repeated myself, "Fuck."

"Hey, look at the bright side. Maybe he's hot."

I laughed. "And gay."

Jeremy added, "And horny."

"And into me," I joked.

Jeremy came over and put a hand on my shoulder. "Well, even if he's an asshole straight dude with bad acne and smelly feet, you can always just come over and hang in my room when you need to get away."

"Thanks, Jeremy," I said. "I just hope he's not an asshole."

"Or needy," he added.

"Or a homophobe."

Jeremy left me to my sorrow about the end of my sweet living situation. And I guessed it was time to vacate the closet on the other side of the room, so I spent the afternoon consolidating everything into my one cramped space. Oh well, I'd done it before for two years—I could do it again.

The next morning as I walked back to my room across the campus, there seemed to be a buzz going around. Clumps of students were all over the quad and all reading the student newspaper. That was odd, because no one usually paid it much mind. In the lobby of the Student Center, I grabbed a copy off the pile near the door. The headline read, 'Men's soccer recruit raises hopes for season.'

I wondered if that was what people were talking about, so I started reading the article.

The men's soccer team has recruited star British forward, Liam Kelsey, who joins a team with sights on a national championship. Kelsey is transferring in his second year and will join team practices immediately.

I really wasn't much of a sports fan, even though my school was always a national contender in multiple sports every year. But as I was going through the doors of the Student Center on my way back to my dorm room, I heard a group of three girls that looked like they were probably freshman all holding copies of the paper. "Oh my gahd, he's so dreamy," said one.

"Have you seen his Instagram? Every post is hot! Did you see his abs," said another as she giggled and held her hand up to her face.

The third was way more blunt than her friends, "I'd fuck him."

Who knew girls talked like that, too? I mean, they don't usually, so this guy must be something extra special. I looked back at the paper. No photo on the front page, but I opened to the jump into the sports section that I usually never read, and there it was. And, holy fuck, those girls were right. Especially the third one. I'd fuck him, too.

Liam Kelsey was so fucking hot. Even though the picture was just his head, so I didn't really know if the girl was right about his body, but those eyes, that hair, that chiseled jawline. He was a total stud. The picture was black and white, but I could tell he had blue eyes, or maybe green. His hair was slightly longer than the typical fashion on an American college campus, but the way it flopped down and almost covered his eyes was hot as fuck.

I decided to sit down on a bench in the middle of the quad for a second. I took out my phone, opened up Insta, and did a quick search for 'Liam Kelsey,' and there it was. I clicked over to his account. He had over 80,000 followers, but that was no surprise. I started scrolling down through his previous posts. Every single one was a thirst trap. Shirtless. Shirtless flexing. Shirtless running. Shirtless in a bathtub with the bubbles strategically positioned to hide just enough.

Then there were the underwear pix. Apparently this kid already had a modeling gig with an expensive brand. Each of these posts were tagged with the name of the brand and featured him. I got a little more excited when the photo would be of him and another dude or a few dudes. They were borderline homoerotic. Total thirst traps. The models would all cross-tag each other and say things like, 'hanging with my boys' or 'follow my bro.' I did take a minute to zoom in on a few of the pix to confirm. OK, yeah, I was checking out the bulges. And I confirmed, sure enough, I was right—blue eyes. But not just typical blue. They were those ocean blue eyes that are almost see-through. The kind you could get lost in. I hoped I would get a chance to bump into him on campus. Before I closed the app, I clicked 'Follow.'

Getting off the elevator on the second floor, I barely took two steps before Jeremy was coming straight at me. "Oh fuck, Daniel. Holy mother fuckin' shit."

"What?" He was freaking me out a little to be honest.

"Have you been in class all morning?"

"Yeah, why?"

"So you don't know," he asked me.

"Know what?"

"I can't. I can't. Just... just go to your room. And find me later," he said.

I went down to the end of the hall, turned the corner, and got to my door. And as soon as I opened it, I knew exactly what Jeremy was freaking out about. Standing in the middle of my room with a bunch of boxes and suitcases was Liam Kelsey.

"Alright, roomy!" He looked at me with a huge smile and those impossibly blue eyes and that floppy black hair. The breath came right out of my lungs.

"Hi..," I squeaked, barely audible. I'm not even sure if he heard it.

Liam stood there wearing a pair of long-ish white athletic shorts and a blue and white, oversized rugby shirt. I just stood there, mouth open. I didn't know what to say.

"Well, are you coming in then," he asked me, which broke the fog in my mind enough for me to come back down to reality.

"Yes, sorry. I didn't expect to see anyone in here. I'm Daniel. I guess you're my new roommate?"

"Good, then. I'm Liam." he said through a giant smile and reached out a hand to grab mine, "So I will have guessed this is my side, since it's empty. No doubt. This is my bed. That's yours. Is that how it is?"

The fog was still lifting from my head, and I dropped my backpack on my small desk, and went to sit on my bed. "Yes. I've been here for a few weeks now. I didn't know I was getting a roommate today."

"Your lucky day, then, isn't it," he would not stop smiling.

"It was nice having it all to myself." Shit, I'm such an asshole. "But yeah, sorry, welcome. I read about you in the paper today." I'm such a dork.

"All good let's hope."

"Oh, yeah, just about you joining the soccer team and all."

"Football."

"What?"

"I guess I'm going to have to get used to that. Soc... cer. Dumb name really."

I laughed finally and let the air out of my lungs for the first time. Liam turned away to the biggest box at the foot of his bed and bent over to pick up. I don't know how close you've ever come to college soccer players, but when he bent over like that, I got a full view of his amazing round bubble butt. I could not stop staring, even when he'd rose back up to put the box down on his bed.

Looking around at me, he caught me looking, smiled at me, and asked, "Are you looking at me bum?"

I stuttered, I faltered, I turned beat red. "What? No. I was... I was just... wondering do you need help with the boxes? I mean, unpacking?"

Liam winked at me and didn't stop smiling, his dimples destroying my stomach which turned over with a thousand butterflies, "Ah, that's all right. But if you don't have anywhere to go, you can keep me company."

"Oh," I said, coming back to earth. "We'll keep each other company more than we'd ever want to with these dorm rooms. Welcome to 200 square feet of paradise." I was finally able to finish a complete sentence with him.

Liam continued to unpack while I pretended to read a textbook. He told me about his trip, his decision to come to the States to play, his mother who was not at all happy about it. He asked me about the campus, where things were, I gave him the lowdown on all the boring stuff like the Student Center, the cafeteria, the library. I could tell he was really appreciating it.

"So, have you met your teammates yet," I asked.

"Oh, no, I haven't. And they've already been practicing for about a month now, is that right?"

"I really have no idea. I'm not a huge sports fan to be honest."

Liam looked over at me with a bit of surprise. "Really? You go to this school, and you're not a fan? Am I supposed to report you to the authorities or anything like that?"

I laughed. "No. But you'll find most people here eat, sleep, and drink the sports teams. I think I'm a bit of an anomaly."

As he finished unpacking his last box, Liam turned to me and asked, "And how are the girls?"

I think I probably turned a whole new shade of red when he asked me that, and I was flustered. Do I just come out first thing and tell him I'm gay? Here he is just finishing unpacking, and he's going to immediately turn around and start refilling all those boxes. But I'm not one for lies.

"Well, actually, I, um, well, I'm gay. So I wouldn't really know."

Liam shot a half smile my way and shrugged. "Oh all right then. Cheers." And after a long pause and a deep silence during which I had no idea if I should say anything or not, he added, "So how are the boys?"

I had to laugh, and when I did, he laughed with me. "Well, to be honest, I wish I could tell you. I haven't had much luck."

"Then they must be blind," he said.

I didn't want to miss this opportunity, so I mustered up the courage and asked him right away, "So you're straight I guess, right?"

Liam sighed and took a moment before replying, "I don't really much go in for labels."

"Oh," I said. I was speechless. He was looking right into my eyes, but before I could say anything more, the door burst open, and five or six guys I didn't know barreled into the room, screaming and hooting. They lunged at Liam, grabbing at him.

"There he is! The new guy," the biggest and loudest one called out. They were all howling like wolves, and two of them lifted Liam off his mattress that he hadn't even made yet. One other guy was fake-punching him in the chest. It didn't take long for me to realize they were from the soccer team.

They flanked him on both sides and started shoving him toward the door. "Let's go then. Time to show you off!"

With barely a few seconds to make any effort, Liam called back to me, "Well, I'm off it seems. You coming?"

I didn't get to answer before they had dragged him away for some jock form of initiation or something. But they were definitely not my kind of crowd, so I didn't follow along. I just sat there on my bed thinking about those eyes, that hair, that butt,...

Every day for a week was the same. I barely ever saw my new roommate. He was always either in class or at practice or maybe he was out getting laid. Everyone on campus was buzzing about him, particularly the girls. The boys were all talking about a national championship. The girls were all talking about how dreamy Liam was. I agreed more with the girls on that, but even though he was my roommate, I didn't get to see much of him.

Jeremy was all over me all the time for details. I only wish I had any. Liam was never in the room much. He slept with shorts and a t-shirt on. He never changed in front of me. He didn't hang out shirtless all the time like his feed would make you assume.

That feed was actually the only place I ever did get to see much of him. Now his posts all looked familiar but very tame. Liam on the campus soccer field. Liam in front of the student center posing with two girls. Liam eating in the cafeteria. Now in his posts, he was Liam the college soccer player and not Liam the shirtless underwear model. So I scrolled back on the history on his feed to get a better look at things. I just wished I could see some of it live in my dorm room.

I had a worried thought that maybe he was avoiding being in our room, because I told him I'm gay. I was lying on my bed, scrolling through some of his older, smoking-hot shirtless pictures one day when I heard him turning the key in the lock. I frantically clicked my phone off so he wouldn't think I was some kind of pervy stalker.

As he stepped in, he saw me, and a big smile bloomed across his face, "There we are now. Roomie, I haven't seen you in so long. How you doing?"

"Oh I'm fine. Same as ever. You must be so busy with the team."

Liam came over and sat on my bed, which I have to admit made my heart jump. "If it's not practice, it's a game. If it's not the team, it's class. I can't wait until the season is over."

"I hear you're on a winning streak."

Liam smiled and tilted his head. I could tell he didn't want to brag, but he had to say, "Undefeated."

"That's awesome. Congrats."

He didn't answer but nudged his shoulder into me once, then rose up, and went to his own side of the room. He dropped his backpack on the floor at the foot of his bed and fell down onto the pillows with his phone. I went back to scrolling social media but made a point to stay off his page in case he were to see me perving over his shirtless pictures.

I heard a click and looked over and saw him taking selfies. He kept changing the angle of his body, where he held the phone, shifted closer to the window, and snapped pic after pic. He'd snap a shot, then review it for a while before taking another one. He sighed with some frustration in the sound.

"Hey roomie," he called out to me.

"Yeah?"

"Would you do me a favor?"

"Sure," I said.

"I know I sound like a total wanker. But would you take my picture?"

I took a deep intake of breath and tried to not sound as eager as I was. "Sure."

He jumped off his bed and moved the small table that sat under our single window. Looking at the light coming in, he decided where he wanted to stand, and handed me his phone.

"OK," he said. "You stand over there. I want to get the lighting right."

"Sure, yeah."

"Try it now."

I clicked a picture of him, and he put his hand out for the phone. He looked at it for a few seconds and said, "No, this isn't working. Can we use your lamp there?" He pointed over at my desk.

"Yeah, OK. Let me get it." As I handed it to him, our fingers touched, and there was a moment where he wasn't pulling the lamp from my hand. He just stood there and looked right into my eyes. His fingers touching mine, his eyes looking right into me, I exhaled, and my cock turned itself on in my pants.

He propped my desk lamp against some books and uplit himself with it. He pointed toward my bed, which I took to mean he wanted me to stand there. He handed me his phone again. I snapped another picture and passed the phone back to him. He looked at it and seemed a little bit more pleased than the last time but said, "No it's just not working."

"Why don't you take your shirt off?" Oh my gahd. Did I just say that? I don't know how I let the words slip from my mouth, but there it was out there now.

"Well, aren't we a little cheeky today?" He gave a little mocking tone to his words. "So you've seen my feed I guess?"

I didn't know if I should admit that I've been looking at his underwear pictures practically every day since I discovered his account, but I finally said, "Well yeah. When I figured out who you are."

"That's fair," he said. "So will you take some pictures for me?"

I nodded, "Sure, it'll be fun."

"OK, this won't make you uncomfortable, will it?"

I couldn't think of anything that would make me more comfortable. "Not at all."

Liam lifted his shirt off, and fuck. There they were, those crazy impressive abs, that chest. He positioned himself in front of the window again. He judged the lighting, then tilted his torso to the side a bit, which made his six-pack flex. I didn't waste the moment and started clicking the camera on his phone. He put a hand behind his head. I took the pic. He looked up and out the window. I took the pic. He leaned against the wall and looked at me with a 'come fuck me' look in his eyes. I took the picture. My cock got even harder.

After we'd taken dozens of different poses, he took his camera back from me. Still looking down at it and without looking at me, he said, "Now you."

My heart stopped. "What?"

"Your turn," he finally looked up at me. This crazy hot underwear model college jock living in this one little room with just me was looking right at me with a devious kind of a smile on his face.

"Take your shirt off," he commanded. I listened.

I went over to the window and tried to pose like he had. But I don't have much experience in front of a camera. I don't have any experience behind one either, but somehow that was much easier. He took a photo of me, and then another, and another.

He sighed as if frustrated. "This isn't working. Come over here." He put out his hand toward me. I walked toward him, and he slid his hand between my torso and my arm. The touch of his hand on my side made me quiver. Every butterfly in the world was suddenly in my stomach doing somersaults. "I want you on my bed."

"What?" I think I shrieked.

"Lie down," he commanded. I obeyed.

I lay on his bed, my head on his pillow. It smelled like a concentrated form of him. I breathed in heavily and hoped he didn't notice. He hovered over me and clicked another picture.

"Put your hands in the elastic there." He pointed at my waistline. I listened, putting three fingers of each hand into the waistband. "Now pull it down a bit."

"Oh fuck yeah, Daniel. Now that is hot." He clicked the camera button several times. "Turn your head to the window." He kept telling me to move here and there, subtle little changes. He had been taking my picture for what felt like an eternity. I was so aroused, there was no way he didn't notice, or maybe he did.

Finally I had to interrupt it all, "OK, OK, you're wasting film," I joked.

I looked up at Liam. Liam the sports star. Liam the underwear model. Liam the British soccer star, or football star, I guess. I was shirtless in his bed. He was shirtless leaning over me. I tilted my head up off his pillow and looked down at his shirtless body. But it wasn't his pecs or his abs that caught my attention. It was the huge raging bulge of a hard-on in his pants. I looked right at it. He looked at me looking right at it.

"Daniel," he said.

"Yeah," I squeaked.

"You have no idea how fucking hot you are, do you?"

I didn't know what to say. I just looked up into the crazy blue eyes, those eyes like a see-through ocean, those eyes that were staring back at me. "Me?" I finally got a word out. "You're the stud underwear model."

"Daniel. I want you. I've wanted you since the first day I got here. So I have one question for you, roomie."

"What?" I asked him.

"Will you let me fuck you?"

There was no word in the English language, either American or British, that I could say except one. "Yes."

Liam lowered down on top of me. His entire beautiful body touching mine from along our intertwined legs, our hips, our raging bulges in our shorts, his stomach and chest on mine, and then he planted his lips on mine and kissed me deeply. One of his hands slipped behind my head. The other wove back around me between my torso and my arm, just like the first time he'd touched me. His tongue darted into my mouth, and he kissed me like I'd always fantasized.

I felt his huge cock rubbing on mine. He added more motion to increase how much contact they had with each other through the fabric of our shorts. He stopped kissing me and leaned his head back up. "Daniel," he said.

"Yeah?"

"This can't be awkward. We still have to be roommates for the rest of the year. Are you sure this is OK?"

I wanted it so much, my entire body was alive with passion. From head to toe, I felt him on me, but I also had some spark of realization in my head about what he said. "Um, I can't think of anything I want more."

Liam looked right at me. "It's only weird if we make it weird."

"I don't want it to be weird."

He smiled, "Neither do I. So take those shorts off before I tear them off of you."

He didn't let me though and reached down and yanked my shorts off of me. Looking up at me, he smiled and said, "Well hello there." He bent further down and, holding my cock in his hand, he put his lips on the head and let it slide into his mouth and down his throat one inch at a time. I let out the largest sigh I had ever sighed in my life. Every bit of oxygen left my lungs as Liam took my entire cock down his throat. By the time he let it slide back out again, I was able to take a breath again. He looked up at me through his jet-black hair that fell down over his face and smiled with my cock still in his mouth.

I could tell he'd done it before. He bobbed up and down on me, letting just enough spit cover my shaft as he stroked it with his hand as each inch came out of his mouth. He kept it up for a while as I lingered there in bliss. Finally he stopped and came back up face to face. Kissing me passionately, I could taste myself on his lips. "Do you have any condoms and lube," he asked.

"In my desk drawer." He got up and retrieved them. Pulling off his shorts, he looked at me again. I looked down at his cock, now freed from the fabric of his shorts as they fell to the floor, and I gasped. He was uncut, which wasn't surprising, being European and all. His cock was long and thick, thicker in the middle, with a big set of balls. It was probably a poster child for all cocks. He bit the package of the condom, pulled it out, and slid it on. Squeezing the lube, he rubbed it all along his wrapped shaft, then reached his hands down between my legs and under my balls. First one finger touched me right on my hole, and I moaned. His lube-soaked finger slid into me, and I smiled up at him. He grinned down at me with a devilish grin before adding a second finger.

"How is that," he asked.

"Perfect," I answered.

He slid his fingers out and kneeled between my legs. He picked them up and put one on each of his shoulders and leaned into me. "I'll take it slow," he said.

I'd only let someone fuck me a few times before that, and my ex-boyfriend wasn't anywhere near as big as Liam. But I was eager and ready and wanted this more than anything. Slowly he eased into me, first one inch, then he let me breathe and relax, before sliding in a little more, then more.

It felt like forever, but Liam was patient. He wanted this, too, I could tell. "Is it all in yet," I asked him.

He turned his head side to side, "A few more inches to go, baby."

"Fuck how many does that make?"

Liam smiled at me, "Eight full plus a little more. You think you can take it all?"

"Every last inch," I sighed. And with that he pushed more, and my ass opened up, and I took his entire shaft in. He moaned as well and planted his lips on mine. As his tongue darted into my mouth, he let half his cock slide back out of me and right back in again. He fell into a passionate rhythm. As his cock slid out of me, he slid his tongue into my mouth. As his tongue retracted, he planted his huge root into my ass.

He started with a slow, passionate rhythm then started to increase it. My ass relaxed completely. It knew what it wanted, and it wanted to get fucked by this hot English soccer jock. Liam could tell I was loving it. I was moaning and staring right into his eyes. And then he turned it on. Suddenly he grabbed both of my ankles and started fucking me hard and fast like a piston engine. His hips started slapping against mine. His huge balls were bouncing against my ass. He had his tongue out between his smiling lips. And I was getting pounded by his huge cock.

He didn't stop. He didn't slow down. He was like an animal getting just what he wanted. I reached up and caressed his chest, trailing my hand down to feel mound after mound of his ridiculous abs. He planted his cock all the way inside me and lowered himself until he was practically lying on top of me. He kept fucking my ass and put his head to my neck and started licking and sucking. I quivered with the passion and the tickling sensation as his tongue rolled all over my neck muscles.

Leaning back up again and putting his face right in front of mine, he looked me in the eyes and sighed, "Oh baby. So is this weird?"

"No," I moaned. "Not at all."

"Good. So we can do this all year," he said before I felt his lower body quiver and shake. His eyes rolled back, and I could feel the pulsing of his cock as he climaxed while still pumping in and out of me.

He pulled out and rolled onto the side of me. I was still rock hard. He grabbed my cock in his hand and stroked it lightly. He leaned over me with that big dimpled smile and stared at me with those dreamy eyes. "Daniel?"

"Yeah?"

"We're not wasting that hard-on. Now it's your turn. Will you fuck me?"

I was so happy with that question, I practically shot my load hearing it. "Fuck yeah I will."

Before I did, as I reached for the box of condoms and put one on, I leaned over Liam, and with my hazel eyes, I looked into his, and I asked, "Unless you think this is going to be weird."

He laughed as I slid my cock into his round, soccer player bubble butt.

And that's basically how the rest of my junior year went. Liam and the soccer team won the national championship, and I lived with the best roommate a guy could hope for in 200 square feet of paradise.

Dorm Dabble

by Eric Del Carlo

These were to be my glory days? I had a gutful of bitterness, a heart filled with unrequited longing, and loins burning with desire that no female within yelling distance seemed interested in satisfying.

I was away at college—away at a party college—and I couldn't get laid to save my life.

I was nineteen, still brimming with post-adolescent horniness. Before packing off to my higher education, I had done pretty damn well with the ladies, even if I do say. My success with romance and casual sex had instilled all the confidence I'd figured I would need to truly cut loose in an environment which allowed—nay, encouraged—profligate behavior. This particular university had a reputation. If you went here, you'd get all the pussy you wanted.

Well, I had the wanting part down pat...

I had no idea what I was doing wrong. I certainly wasn't a sleaze or a creep. Enough women had previously complimented me on my looks—even on my dick size—to make me believe I was a worthy male specimen. I'd learned charm, manners. I avoided pushiness, desperation, vulgar conduct. No part of me wanted to "trick" a woman into bed, or play head games, or manipulate anyone in any way. I was proud to be sexually woke, and simply wished to enter fully into the carnal arena and enjoy that ultimate human experience while my body was still a ripe and taut engine and I could get a hard-on just by thinking a few delicious dirty thoughts.

But for whatever reason, I was caught in a cycle of continuous failure. There wasn't even a pattern to it. I socialized as much as I could, and when what looked like an opportunity arose for me, I would make an overture to some female. And get turned down. Politely. Gently. But immediately and without room for reprieve.

I'd go to an off-campus party, for which this school was infamous, and find myself dancing with some breathtaking hottie. I would then try to convert our sensual intimacy on the dance floor into a first negotiated step toward a different kind of physical closeness.

"Oh." Eyes blinking rapidly in a pretty face. "Oh. Sorry. No. You're a good dancer, Dirk, but—"

It was like I wasn't even in the running, like I was some category of male one wouldn't ever consider fooling around with.

I didn't understand it. But I kept bucking myself up, again and again, muttering ridiculous aphorisms at the mirror, telling myself I was good enough, handsome enough, and gosh darn it surely somebody wanted to fuck me!

But reality slapped my face over and over. There was no dearth of women at the school. The split was about fifty/fifty, in fact. But if there were a statistical pool of happily frisky women out there who might find me attractive—or at least passable—they were an elusive breed. Or, as seemed more and more likely, they didn't actually exist at all.

I trudged back to the dorm room I shared with Antonio. With nothing else to occupy me I was pouring my energy into my schoolwork. Celibacy was probably going to end up being good for my GPA, but it was a sad tradeoff. If I'd been getting regular—or even some sex—my mind would be more at ease and my classroom work and assignments easier to handle, I figured.

As it was, it felt like I was dragging around a weight with me all day. I felt...embarrassed. It was a secret shame, at least. Nobody was pointing me out on campus and saying, "Born-again virgin!" But I still felt singled out, or more accurately left out. Because, goddamnit, everyone else seemed to be having the time of their lives.

So, it was par for the fucking course when I walked into our dorm room and found Antonio wearing nothing but his skintight briefs, earbuds in, dancing his familiar "victory" dance.

Yep. Of course. My dear dorm buddy had gotten laid. Again.

I liked Antonio. He was a cool guy. And he wasn't doing his dance to rub my face in anything. Also, who was I to begrudge him the kind of sexual success I so desperately wished were mine?

But this, today, was like the last damn straw. There was a giant, orgiastic gala going on all around me at this school, but my invitation had gotten lost in the mail. I was so sick of sneaking away to jerk off while everyone else got to have legitimate, grown-up, carefree sex.

Antonio had his eyes closed as he gyrated. He was mouthing words, face bright with obvious postcoital smugness. I hoped—bitterly—that he'd gotten his rocks off but good. I hoped he'd fucked like a bull. I hoped—

His eyes opened, and his underwear dance froze in mid-step. He gave me an ear-to-ear grin and popped out his earbuds.

"Dirk!"

I threw my laptop down on my bed and felt like throwing myself face down on the floor. Instead I said, "I suppose congratulations are in order."

He shrugged nonchalantly, and that just made it worse, but he couldn't have known that. I'd been withholding most of the bad luck I'd been having from him. Again, I was embarrassed, especially because Antonio—no better looking than me, no more charming, I thought—was having the kind of carnal adventures I had been hoping for at the start of the school year.

"Hey," he said, "it was just a little rumpy-pumpy."

The cute name didn't make the sting of jealousy go away any faster for me. "Well, I hope it was a good time." I managed not to grind my teeth audibly as I said it.

"Nothing like pounding ass to set the world right."

Wonderful. He'd gotten anal. How happy I was for him. Bastard. "Sounds...fun."

He laughed. "Yeah, he's fun all right."

Now it was my turn to freeze. He? Antonio had said...?

Something passed over his eyes. He must have realized what he'd just said, what he had let slip. I had thought all his recent sex partners were women. When we'd first met, he had talked about past girlfriends. Had all that been a smoke screen?

For a moment he looked anxious, then he shrugged.

"You were with a guy?" I asked.

He let out a breath. "Yeah, Dirk. I was." He peered at me. "Is that going to be a problem for you?"

We'd shared this snug little room for months. Antonio was easy to be around. I counted him as a friend. "Hell no," I countered. "You think I'm a homophobe?"

"I think," he said, quietly, "that people who live together ought to be okay with one another."

"Antonio. Cross my heart, hope to die. If you're gay, it's fine with me. Or bi. Or any other category of sexual identification you'd care to name that doesn't involve animals or children. It just caught me off-guard. So. You want to tell me about this 'fun' guy you were with?" Maybe it would be easier knowing my dormmate was having queer sex.

Antonio sat on his bed. He had a trim, decently muscled body. His physique was a lot like mine.

"His name's Xander. He—well, what do the details matter? I want to tell you something, Dirk, but I want to ask a question first. Can I?"

"Sure." I sat on my bed. We faced each other across the small space.

He asked, "Have you ever had sex with a male?"

"Nope."

"Ever done anything? Kissed a boy? Let yourself get groped in a park, anything?"

I shook my head.

He sighed. "I hadn't either. Oh, I'd thought about it from time to time, and there had been opportunities. But I realize now that I didn't follow through on any of those chances not because I was hopelessly and forever heterosexual, but because I was chickenshit!"

It startled a nervous laugh out of me.

He nodded. "I wish I'd tried it. I wish I'd had a boyfriend in high school. Look, I liked the girls I dated. I liked their moving parts. But...Jesus, Dirk...there's a whole other side to sexuality. I wasn't homophobic either, but I think we both had the same kind of upbringing, and we absorbed more needless bullshit than we'd care to admit to. Like the notion that gay sex doesn't 'count.' I got rid of one little hang-up and boom. My sex life is off the charts now. I've got half a dozen dudes around school I go to for hassle-free sex. It's awesome!"

Half a dozen? I tried—and failed—to imagine myself with six different sex partners. The jealousy came back, but it was a new variety for me. I was jealous of my friend's numerous male lovers!

I was also brimming with curiosity. All of a sudden I wanted to ask him questions. "But—is it just getting off? I mean, when I've been with women, it's not just the orgasm that counts. I dig the whole thing, the sensuality of the experience, their looks, touching them. You don't...uh...mind that with a guy?"

He looked like he was going to make some snap reply. Then he got a reconsidering look on his face. "Actually, that's a fair question. At first—not gonna lie—I was nervous. It felt weird. I definitely liked what I was doing, but I didn't really trust myself. I guess I had some stupid misgivings to get over, more of that bad societal programming. I can tell you now, though, that I'm totally over any apprehensions. It's like I've discovered delicious food I never knew existed. Or I'm hearing soaring music that I never encountered before. I'm not even saying I'm full-on gay. I seriously doubt I've fucked my last female. But I am so enjoying this queer sex thing."

I still had questions. They coursed through my head, ranging from the philosophical to the purely mechanical. By now I had fully absorbed my dormmate's new sexual status. It wasn't exactly exotic, after all. I'd had gay acquaintances back in high school.

I started blurting my further questions, one after the other, barely pausing to let Antonio begin to answer. Finally he put up a hand, an indulgent smile on his face.

"Look. Dirk. Ol' buddy, ol' pal. What I'm hearing is a lot of, well, interest on your part. I'm glad you're cool with my lifestyle. If you weren't, I would've seriously misjudged you. But..." He flashed a provocative grin. "If you really want to know what it's like..."

"We shouldn't fuck," I said, bluntly, gracelessly, the words just popping out.

He looked surprised, then laughed. "No. We shouldn't. Dormmates should probably never do that. And I'm not offering. However, if you're more than curious about all this, I can set you up with someone. One of the guys I know likes skinny muscled males, like I am, like you are. He's easygoing. He gives great head. He's a wicked fun lover. If you want a hookup of the male variety, you say so. His name is Gareth."

We left it at that.

Antonio went out. I lay on my bed. Stared at the ceiling. Listened to my heart's rapid beats. And I thought it all the way through.

* * *

I kept on thinking it through for a week. I weighed my established sexuality (Dirk MacAfee likes girls) against my maddening dry spell (Dirk has been without pussy too long) and came to no definite conclusions.

I tried being coldly rational. I tried going with my gut. I also gave the women on campus another go, but I was like the loser kid at a dance who didn't know he had no chance of scoring.

The bitterness overwhelmed me. All the while Antonio's generous offer played in my mind. My friend was willing to share a lover with me, without hint of jealousy, asking nothing of me in return. Was that how things normally ran with gay men? Not that Antonio was completely gay—so he claimed—but...

I was hung up. It was an ugly little realization. I could spout all the proclamations of woke inclusive attitudes I wanted, but underneath was some of that nasty societal programming Antonio had mentioned. Some stupid part of me thought that queer sex wasn't as—I don't know—proper or meaningful or something as "regular" sex.

After all, this Gareth was willing to get me off with no strings attached. At least according to Antonio. Instinct told me my dormmate wouldn't have dangled a lover in front of me if he wasn't sure.

And goddamn, I was horny.

Finally, I spoke the words to Antonio: "I'd like to hook up with Gareth."

To his credit Antonio didn't gloat. He simply sent a text, waited, and two minutes later looked up from his phone and said, "It's on."

Gooseflesh went up both my arms. My gut did a roller coaster flip. This, then, was going to be a completely new experience in my youngish life. I was nervous. I was excited.

Gareth dwelled in a different block of dorms. In a daze I crossed the campus. Everything seemed preternaturally bright. The leaves on the trees looked like glass. The clouds in the sky were all Impressionist paintings. I breathed air that felt crisp and clean in my lungs.

I stood at Gareth's door a long, tense, breathless moment. I might well chicken out, right here, right now. And if I did, I knew I would never try something like this again.

There was a tingling through my loins. My heart skipped a fast tempo. My palms were sweaty. The physical/sexual side of me wanted this. Needed this. I craved contact. Contact and release. Please. Give me that.

So I knocked on the door.

Three seconds and about six quick heartbeats passed.

The door opened. There stood Gareth. This had to be Gareth. I realized only now that Antonio hadn't described him physically.

He was about my height, my build, maybe even a little tauter. His blondish hair was buzzed on the sides and stood up in artful tufts atop his head. Blue eyes, like gemstones underwater. Easy features which now split into a smile. As I stood silent, he'd looked me up and down.

"Well, if you're not Dirk, I'm just going to pretend you are." He stepped back, inviting me in.

My feet felt glued down. "I'm Dirk," I said. Every bit of awkwardness I had felt with women over the past months suddenly was crashing down on me. Without even entering this man's dorm room, I was already completely off my gyros. What was I doing here? What made me think I belonged here?

Hetero programming, idiot, I told myself. Any awkward feelings are your own doing.

"Then come on in, Dirk, and close the door before you let out all the gay," he tittered, turning away, leaving me to decide what to do.

I "bravely" stepped across the threshold and pushed the door shut behind me. I saw that he occupied a single—one bed, one desk. It was a neat space with posters on the walls.

I unclenched my jaw. "We have a mutual friend."

Gareth turned. He wore a jersey and sweatpants. "Antonio's a little more than a friend. Or a little less. Whichever. He's a nice boy. I like sucking his cock. Do you want yours sucked?"

He was playing. This was all utterly casual to him. The smile stayed on his face, but there was no real mockery in it.

I'd been asked a question. The question. My chin jerked up and down, as if yanked by a wire. I didn't trust my voice.

"Good," Gareth said. "Because I'm in the mood for a taste."

With that he peeled off the jersey. As he hooked his thumbs into the waistband of his sweats, I blurted, "What're you doing?" my voice just as quivery as I'd feared.

He didn't stop, stepping naked out of the sweatpants and flinging them aside. He had a swimmer's body, all lean sinew and tight proportions but not grossly muscular. I realized—on a very distant, almost abstract level—that this seemed to me a good physique for a male. Attractive. Alluring.

His cock dangled. His blond pubic hair was buzzed as well, and that too looked... aesthetic.

Gareth put his hands on his bare hips, utterly unself-conscious about his nudity. "Well, Dirk, darling. I plan to blow you. Now, you're not going to come in my mouth, so when you shoot off, your jizz is going to go flying. I don't want it on my clothes...but I certainly don't mind warm splatters of boy-juice on my bare skin. Get it? Got it?"

What do I say to that? I just nodded again, aware that my cock was stirring and desperately trying not to self-analyze that too heavily.

I asked, "Do I get naked too?"

"If you want. At any rate, I'm going to need to see your dick." He was both impish and matter-of-fact.

Was I supposed to sit in a chair, lie on the bed? I didn't want to ask another question. I thumbed open my jeans, slid my briefs down a bit, and hauled out my thickening cock. I was trembling and hoping I was hiding it. I'd been nude in front of men in locker rooms and gym showers, but this—obviously—was a whole different scenario.

I stood where I was. Gareth padded forward and gracefully knelt in front of me. My cock twitched, still growing. His blue eyes fastened to it, and some of the mirth left his face, replaced by a gleam of lust which I could only find gratifying.

Something rang in the back of my brain, a revelation: there was no possibility—in my life, anyway—of a woman ever doing this. Not without a great many preliminaries. Not without sensible examination of me, testing my character, making sure I wasn't a creep. More, making certain I was worthy of something as precious and intimate and, frankly, one-sided as a blowjob.

I'd gotten my cock sucked before, but it had never been anywhere near as easy as this setup was playing out to be. Five minutes ago I had knocked on this guy's door. Now he was kneeling naked before me, ready to wrap his mouth around my swollen, purple knob!

He murmured something. I didn't catch it, but it sounded appreciative. Then I felt his hot breath on my cockhead, and as I continued to stand there, a shiver at the core of my being, I drew air sharply through my bared teeth as his tongue unfurled and swiped itself over my round, sensitive crown.

I had to plant my feet firmer on the rug. This was happening. This was happening! All the exciting aspects and all the unfamiliar/scary ones were necessarily giving way to the male mouth now closing around me. I looked down and watched Gareth's lips seal themselves over my cockhead. I felt his tongue still wriggling. Then, like this were the best magic trick in the world, I beheld in wonder as his head moved forward and my cock disappeared from view. He sucked me all the way down, in one smooth lunge, with a lovely growl in his throat. His blue eyes rolled up into his head as if he were experiencing something so succulent, so beautiful, it made him want to swoon.

Damn, his mouth felt good. I saw the caved-in cheeks, felt the luscious suction. My cockhead was in his throat. If this man had a gag reflex, it was one he could apparently turn off at will.

His hand tugged my briefs further down, so he could cradle my balls. The soft pressure added to the sweet sensation of oral stimulation. ("Oral stimulation"? Really? Are we that clinical? This was a talented mouth on my cock, and I should let myself enjoy it.)

He started to lift and drop his mouth. The ring of his lips didn't falter. He slid up and down on my vein-lined shaft. Spit glistened on me. Gareth sucked me to the root each time. I watched my dark curls brushing his nose and hoped I wasn't too unshowered for him.

That savoring look never left his features. He softly, rhythmically squeezed my balls. His speed increased. The suction stayed tight.

I was getting my cock sucked by a man. I allowed myself this last detached observation. The episode would be a demarcation in my life. Before it, purely heterosexual high jinks. After, I would be a male who'd had carnal congress with another male. Would I be noticeably changed? Even to myself?

Right now I didn't care. This felt too fucking good. I needed this so badly. Here was a fellow human being who found me desirable enough to perform this coveted sex act on me. I should be—and was—grateful.

Gareth kicked into another gear. He was going to town now. He made urrmmm sounds as he sucked me.

"Stop!" I gasped. The word was out suddenly. My thoughts tumbled, trying to catch up. Why did I want him to—"I want to be naked too," I added hastily.

Gareth sat back on his haunches as I did a vaudeville routine of a man stripping. Managing not to completely pratfall, I kicked off my last stitch and faced my friendly cocksucker in a state of absolute undress. My flesh was hot. My forehead was slick with sweat.

He moved neatly back into place and resumed sucking me off. I put my hands to his head, feeling the stiff thistles of his hair, and dared to meet his mouthy plunges with pelvic thrusts. He took my strokes expertly, never breaking stride.

Heat rolled up me. The air crackled. I felt my come forming, taking its time, then deciding all at once to move forward. Pleasure was roiling all through me. I was about to open my mouth, to tell him I was near the brink, but his hand on my balls was apparently all the gauge he needed.

He took me to the edge, to the frantic precipice. Abruptly his mouth whipped away, and as he panted, his other hand worked my slick staff. One pump. Two. Three—

I erupted. It was a climax from the soles of my feet to the apex of my skull. I unloaded hard. The first spurt hit Gareth right at the notch of his neck. Gooey pearl ooze splattered. Fierce spews followed. I came on his swimmer's pecs. My cum dribbled down his chest and belly.

Rapture consumed me. The intensity was incredible. Maybe it was the release of all the tension. Maybe Gareth was really just that good a sucker of cock. In the dazed afterglow I was inclined to believe the latter.

I staggered back. He let go of my slickened cock.

I had to say something. "Jesus, dude. You suck so good."

He smirked. "Actually, I suck well. You just got blown by an English major, my dear." He ran his fingers over his chest and stomach, smiled at the pearlescent gloop he'd collected. He reached for a hand towel stashed under the bed and wiped himself off.

I said, "Is there anything I can...do for you?" Again I had spoken before my thoughts had fully formed. The blowjob had razed me down to my instincts, it seemed. I was fidgety, wiry. I felt good, glad, but I didn't feel like this scene was done.

Gareth gazed up at me, wryly. He finished cleaning himself.

"Antonio said you were a man-on-man virgin."

I blushed. Holy shit, I was embarrassed by that? That demarcating change in my life was happening all right. "Yeah. Well, so what? You got a hard-on." I pointed, like his state needed pointing out. "Maybe I should do something about that?"

I hadn't wanted that to come out as a question, but there it was. I was asking his opinion, asking for guidance. He was my first male lover, and I wanted to know if I was supposed to leave this room or stay.

The part of me that wanted to stay was a new part. It was the part that wasn't afraid of shit. It was also a part which evidently felt deep gratitude toward this man, a gratefulness willing to express itself in...well, I wasn't sure what. But I was ready to try something new.

He stood. "You want to suck some cock, sweetheart?" he asked, crooningly, plainly giving me the chance to back off if I wished. But the gleam was in his gem-like blue eyes once more, that hard shine of lust. His cock had become fully erect while he'd blown me.

"No," I said. "Not some cock. Your cock." There, Dirk, you've said it. You've gone halfway queer today, and it's been—let's be honest—fucking awesome. Now go the rest of the way.

Gareth peered at me, as if seeing me differently. I felt, well, exposed. More than just nude. I had made an admission I wouldn't have thought myself capable of even a week ago. It wasn't like I had been living a repressed, closeted life. I had just never appreciated this whole other sexual territory. It was no wonder Antonio was giddy about it all. This was kid-in-a-candy-store stuff.

Putting out his hand, Gareth said softly, "Come here."

I took his hand. He gently led me to the bed. He lay down, drew me down next to him. We lay together. Our bodies pressed. I was intensely aware of the masculinity of him, the hardness of muscle. There was even a faint male scent, something underneath the lingering bouquet of my semen. Gareth snaked an arm around me. He held me close. My muscles went loose, and I snuggled against him. His hard cock was a bar across my thigh.

Excitement remained, despite the fact that I'd just shot my load. But my breathing slowed, and a strange quietude drifted over me. This was...cozy. I didn't feel out of place now. My self-consciousness had retreated.

I started to reach for him, for his cock. Then I asked, "It's okay if I touch you?"

"More than okay, Dirk."

Dirk now. Not sweetheart. Not darling. He was taking me a little more seriously.

I put my hand on him, another first for me. I gently closed my fingers around his shaft, mesmerized by the texture of him, by his dual firmness and softness. It shouldn't be such a surprise, I thought ruefully. Christ knew I'd handled my own cock often enough, especially lately. But it was a different order of things, apparently, to touch another man's junk.

He was warm in my grip. He breathed a sigh against my hair. I shifted and raised my eyes to him. I squeezed him a bit tighter. Tentatively I moved my hand, a single slow pump. It wasn't like jerking myself—the angle was different. But I certainly understood the principles.

"That's nice," he murmured.

I pulled on him some more. The rhythm was right there, waiting. My elbow felt fluid. I sensed I could jack him all the way to a come. But I had promised him something else.

As if aware of my thoughts, he said, "You can just keep doing that."

"I said I want to suck you."

"Okay, then. Who am I to argue?" Humor again, but a hoarseness had come into his voice. He was truly aroused. I was getting him worked up in a major way.

Suddenly I leaned in and kissed him on the lips. He kissed me back. It was sweet and tender, no tongues, but not a chaste kiss. There. I'd kissed a dude. Might as well wrap my mouth around his cock, too, I thought with giddy abandon.

I pushed up onto my elbows and started squirming my way down the bed. I looked up at him again. "Feel free to give me pointers." Then I was slipping down between his legs, feeling firm thighs close on my shoulders.

Seconds later I was in the classical position, hunkered betwixt his legs—the blower this time, not the blowee. His cock reared up before my face. I could see every squiggly vein, the thick cap of his cockhead, the seam bisecting his shaved balls.

I felt no alarm. No—for want of a better word—repugnance. I thought about how Gareth had handled me. I mentally reviewed all the blowjobs I had received from women. It wasn't a long list. I grasped the basics, certainly.

I put a hand on Gareth's smooth balls. Again, I felt heat, stirring. How alive he was! How electric this whole situation was. As thrilling as any hetero sex I'd had. And the newness made it an adventure for me.

I just hoped I wouldn't fuck it up.

My mouth hovered over his cockhead. I opened up and put my tongue out. A final glint of hesitation came and vanished. I licked the fleshy plum, swirling it all around, even flicking my tongue tip through his piss-slit. A muscle jumped in his left thigh, and he grunted.

Okay, I told myself. Now to swallow this bad boy...

Again as if hearing his cue, Gareth said, "You want to tuck your teeth just behind your upper and lower lips. Enamel is not your friend in a blowjob."

I followed his sensible instructions.

"Now just put your mouth around me, and slide forward slowly. Use your tongue on me if you want. Ah. Ah, fuck! That's real nice. Don't rush it. Stop when you need to. Breathe through your nose, but get deep breaths..."

It was all helpful. At the same time I was overwhelmed with the tactile sensations. His texture again! It was magnified by my tongue. I wondered how many nerve endings and receptors and whatnot were concentrated in the mouth, making any oral experience a drastic one.

And his flavor. Christ, I had the taste of him on my tongue. Male. Living. A faint sting of soap. I was descending his shaft, the ring of my lips maintaining their seal. I applied suction, flattening my cheeks on him. I heard him gasp. Too much! I eased, savoring what I was doing. My tongue plucked at the tiny veins lining him.

He throbbed in my mouth. Incredible. I had a mouthful of bona fide cock, and I was loving it.

Then I met trouble. Once more, Gareth was Johnny-on-the-spot about it.

"That's your gag reflex. You should stop right there. Back off if you want...or hold there. Let your throat muscles adjust. They will if you let them."

I didn't want to leave him half-sucked, not after the masterful deep-throating he'd given me. But the bulb of his cockhead had reached the back of my throat and my body rebelled. A twinge of panic hit. I was choking! No, I wasn't. I concentrated on muscles I'd never been consciously aware of before. My throat had tried to close, stirring my gorge dangerously. The last thing I wanted was to puke like an amateur.

It took effort. My eyes watered a little. But the cinch of muscles eased. I was soon comfortable with the swollen knob lodged where it was. I could still breathe. Deep breaths through the nose, like he'd advised.

Once I felt wholly secure, I pushed forward. A centimeter. Another one. That lovely round crown was sliding into the drain of my throat. I held off the animal fear in favor of the joy of accomplishing this daunting carnal task.

Gareth groaned as I sucked him all the way down. My nose flattened against the burring stubble of his shaven pubes. A great sense of triumph suffused me. I had conquered this.

Now all that remained was to ride my mouth on him until he spewed his load.

I set off to make that happen, my own body thrumming, a rapture seething in my being.

I'd been hyper-mindful of my teeth and hadn't once grazed him. I kept up that caution as I drew my encircling mouth up to his knob, then plunged back down again, this time with gusto, sure I could bypass my gag reflex.

I managed it, and the next downward lunge was even easier. Soon I had a rhythm going and felt the sweet strain in my neck and back. This was work! But fun work.

Gareth's legs went slack. I massaged his balls as I sucked, and he rewarded me with satisfied moans. Here was an experienced gay sex enthusiast, and I was making him moan. Nice.

With my head rising and falling, a mediative mood came over me. It occurred that none of this felt askew anymore. I was engaged in a flagrant queer sex act—it was one thing to get sucked, another entirely to do the sucking—but there were no lingering traces of guilt or anxiety or any emotional negativity whatsoever. This was purely celebratory.

Spit ran from the corner of my mouth. I was aware that I was getting hard again. I rubbed on the bedding, letting that minor pleasure translate itself into the major pleasure I was giving Gareth.

My speed had picked up. I was going into that final overdrive, mouth flashing up and down his erect shaft. His thighs came back up and started tightening around my sides. His balls stirred under my caressing hand.

Suddenly his hips bucked. He thrust upward, and his cockhead invaded my throat with extra force. I stayed with him, determined, taking his inches. A cry was rising from him, going upward through the octaves. A warbling sound of runaway excitation, of oncoming ecstasy.

Sweat basted my forehead again, my chest. My neck muscles ached. My wriggling tongue was tired. But I would see this through to the spurting end.

Three, four, five more plunges, then Gareth cried out, "I'm gonna shoot!"

At that I wrenched my mouth away, swooped a hand over his staff, and pumped him like mad. One, two, three—He came in a fucking geyser, shooting his jizz onto his belly and chest. A particularly energetic fleck landed on his cheek as his face contorted in hardcore bliss.

Gareth recovered slowly. Finally he pronounced, "Jesus Christ," which I took to be heartfelt approval of my nascent oral ministrations.

He wiped himself off with the towel, then we nuzzled together in postcoital fellowship. We kissed again. Several times. I was still halfway hard, and I had the feeling Gareth would be quick to regroup. Maybe this afternoon of exploration and discovery wasn't over yet.

He murmured, "You okay?"

I tightened my arm over his chest. "More than okay." I held my breath a moment. "Um, is it too soon to wonder if we'll see each other again? You know...like this."

He squeezed my shoulder. "I'd love to see you again, Dirk. Like this. And a whole lot of other ways like this."

I sighed with pleasure. My world had changed today. This, then, was more than just a dabble. I had dared to explore my queer side, and I'd discovered a rich and lovely region there, and I would sprint its fields and romp in its meadows for as long as I liked.

Tag, I'm It!

by Brady P. Books

My fraternity had a tradition of playing an intense game of Tag that lasted a week. It was so much fun. But the game during my junior year is the one I will never forget. For more reasons than the fact that I almost lost.

The rules were simple. At a Saturday night party, usually after most of my brothers were either tired or tipsy, the president of the frat, that year it was Tyler, would stand up and hold this ratty stuffed animal that we called Tagger. He would announce that the game of tag was starting. Whoever had Tagger was 'It.' If you had Tagger, you had to pass him on to one of the other frat brothers by making them touch him. You could not refuse to take Tagger if you were tagged, and there's no tag-backs.

The game would last a week, and on the next Thursday night, whoever had Tagger was crowned the loser. Trust me, you didn't want to be the loser. Guys concocted all sorts of elaborate schemes to pass Tagger on to another brother. As long as the other brother came into contact with Tagger, he was It and was required to take possession of the ratty animal.

Guys have been known to throw Tagger into a guy's face in the middle of the cafeteria, leave him in their gym bag in the fitness center, and when he reaches in after his workout, they jump out from behind the lockers and yell, Tagger! You're It!

Last year, Jimmy, one of my brothers, enlisted the help of this hot cheerleader Stacey. He had her invite my buddy Josh over to her dorm room. She put Tagger under her skirt, and when she took his hand and put it under her skirt, Jimmy, who had been It, jumped out of her closet and yelled, Tagger! You're It! Josh was super embarrassed, but not so much that he didn't tell me the story. Jimmy told everyone else.

Any way, it goes on for almost a full week, from Saturday to Thursday. It's the only week you avoid your brothers like the plague. After that Saturday night at the party, you lose track of who is It. So the whole week, you're on pins and needles all over campus, waiting for a brother to pounce and throw a teddy bear in your face and yell those words, Tagger! You're It!

So like I said, you don't want to be the last one It on Thursday night. At that party, it usually starts at a brother's apartment or dorm room but then ends up roaming all over campus. You see, whoever is left as It with Tagger must do whatever his frat brothers tell him to do. The president and the other board members usually take charge and order It to perform embarrassing things, like carry a plastic cup full of water across campus in nothing but their underwear and fill a bucket outside the freshman dorm. So it takes a lot of trips back and forth. Crowds usually gather and razz the It.

Last year my friend Curtis ended up It. Johnny was president last year, but he was a senior and graduated. Johnny made Curtis put on this weird pair of neon underwear that didn't cover his ass and a lacey bra. He had to wear it all night. We started out parading him across campus to get spectators, but during the entire parade, we all kept spraying Curtis with water guns. Johnny and the other heads of the frat all had these colored powders that they tossed at him.

When we got in front of the freshman dorm, there were a bunch of freshmen that came out to see what we were doing. Johnny said that if you were It, even freshmen were above you. He handed out markers to several young freshmen guys and gave them permission to write all over Curtis. Someone put our Greek letters across his forehead. Somebody wrote Loser in big letters across his chest. Then someone wrote Enter Here on his lower back and an arrow pointing at his ass crack.

Then Curtis was made to stand under the row of hallway windows at the end of the dorm. They gave him a plastic cup and told him to put it on his head. Johnny made him stand against the wall and told him he could leave when the cup was full. From above, the windows opened up, and people started dumping water and soda and beer and sports drink out of the windows. It all splashed down all over Curtis. We were all laughing, including Curtis. He was drenched and sticky and filthy by the time that cup was full.

So like I said, you don't want to end up It. I was determined not to go through what Curtis did the last year. And Scott, who was now a senior, the year before that. Now that I was a junior, I was a little more relaxed, because it's the brand, new freshman brothers and the sophomores that really have the targets on their backs.

So Tyler stood on that table and announced the start of the game. He made this freshman kid Mark come forward and accept Tagger, making him the first It. Typically, Tagger ends up trading hands over and over and over that first night while we're all together. At some point he's just thrown around the room, and people end up screaming about who touched him last. And as the night winds down, people try to figure out who leaves with Tagger, then avoid them the next day. Then it is constant text messages about who has him for the rest of the week.

I texted Curtis, telling him I was committed to not have to go through what he had the previous year. He said it wasn't really all that bad, because for weeks afterward, he got laid a bunch of times by girls who felt bad for him. But he said if he ended up It late in the week, he really wanted to target Tyler, who had made him It in the very last minutes of the week last year.

I thought, good luck with that. Tyler as president enlisted the entire board to protect him. Tyler had two other seniors with him almost every hour of the week. And he lived in senior housing which was the best dorm on campus. They had a front desk security guard who would not allow you in unless you lived there.

My goal was simple. Avoid my frat brothers at all cost. It was hard, because they were my best buds, too. So the week trudged on with not much to do and the constant fear of having a ratty teddy bear thrown in your face.

As the week progressed, I got a steady stream of texts about who was It now, and how they got tagged. Mark the freshman ended up with Tagger at the end of the Thursday night party after all. He tagged this other freshman dude who then threw it at Curtis in the middle of a class. They both ended up getting thrown out by the professor.

Curtis told me he tagged this kid Jason on Monday night. We lost track of It for a while until Tuesday night when the story came out that Brian, this Irish sophomore, flung it at Alvy while he was naked in the dorm showers. He jimmied the door open to his shower stall and threw it right at him yelling, 'Tagger you're It!'

Wednesday I was on full alert. It was definitely fun to be It during the week, which I so far had avoided this entire year. You get to decide who you're gonna target, then try to come up with an elaborate plan to surprise them with it. A good Tag can become legend in the frat. But by Wednesday, there was no fun in being tagged. It started to get stressful the closer to the end of the game it got.

But as luck would have it, there I was walking back to my dorm Wednesday after dinner when I saw Josh coming toward me on the sidewalk. I stopped about twenty-five feet away from him or so. He caught sight of me, and he froze, too. We stood there a distance from each other, staring each other down.

"Are you It," I called over to him.

"No, are you," he asked me.

"No."

"How can I believe you," he screamed over. He put his hands up in the air. I did the same. We both seemed to relax and joined each other to talk. "Dude, do you have any idea who's It?"

"No. Last I heard It was Alvy last night."

"Nah," Josh said. "That's like two or three rounds ago. Alvy tagged Skeet.

"No way, he tagged a senior," I was surprised. "How'd he do it?"

Josh shook his head. "I think he snuck into the senior dorm. Maybe he just knocked on his door and threw it at him or something."

Just then we saw Brian and Curtis coming our way. We stared them down. They stopped and put their hands in the air while shaking their heads. They came up to us, and we continued trying to figure out who was It. Curtis turned to me and said, "Bobby, you haven't been It all week, have you?"

I shrugged, "So far so good," and put my fingers up and crossed them.

"Man," he said. "I do not want to end up It again. That fucking sucked."

Scott immediately backed him up, "Dude, me too. We should get immunity or shit like that."

Curtis looked really nervous. "No way I'm ending up It two years in a row. I don't care if I did get laid last year. Not fucking worth it. I couldn't get that marker off for like a week. My dad saw it on my back. It took like a week to convince him I'm not gay."

Josh said, "So who had Tagger last? Anybody know?"

Curtis answered, "All I know is, I fucking want to figure out a way to make Tyler It."

Scott agreed with him, "Totally. So we should make a pact. If any of us end up being It, we'll protect each other, and we will target Tyler. Deal?"

Josh and Curtis both said, "Deal."

They looked at me. I didn't have anything against Tyler. In fact, I kinda liked him. But if they were offering me a four-person pact to be safe, I had to agree. So I nodded and said, "Yeah totally."

Curtis smiled and looked right at me. "Good deal," he said. "Then we all agree we go after Tyler."

And with that, he pulled his knapsack around and reached into it. Before I could react, Josh and Scott had wrapped their arms around mine and held me in place. Curtis pulled Tagger out of his backpack and shoved it into my face. I tried to pull back, but with two strong frat brothers holding me, all I could do was accept having a stuffed animal smeared all over my face. Curtis then pulled my sweatpants out and pushed Tagger into the elastic waistband.

All three of them jumped away from me. They pointed back at me standing there with a teddy bear in my pants. As they put more and more distance between us, they stared back at me and laughed while they called out, "Tagger! You're It!"

Fuck it was Wednesday. I only had a day to get rid of this thing. In my head I thought I really don't care who I pawn this off on, deal or not. But within a few minutes of getting back to my dorm room, my phone started dinging.

Scott. Remember our deal.

Curtis. Get Tyler.

Josh. Sorry buddy they made me.

I created a group text with just the three of them. OK, I typed. I'll try to get Tyler. But if it gets late tomorrow I'm just gonna Tag anybody I can.

Curtis. Get Tyler! Dude!

Back in my room, I took a better look at Tagger. It was probably originally a bear, but after years of wear and tear, there were only clumps of fluff left here and there. The face was pretty much down to a black, plastic nose and one eye hanging on by a thread. The limbs flopped loosely, and the whole thing was held together by random attempts to keep it in one piece over the years. Some twine, several attempts at sewing by college dudes who didn't know how to sew. Until last year, Tagger wore an eyepatch over the missing googly eye, but that was gone now. I didn't want to know what all the crusty stains were, but I had a guess.

I knew I just wanted to get rid of this no matter what. But I also thought, if I could successfully tag Tyler, I would be a legend. I decided Wednesday night would be my only chance. Thursday it was free game on any brother I could find.

I waited until later that night and texted my brothers. So any idea where Tyler would be?

Curtis texted me back on a private DM. Dude, he's in his room in the senior dorm.

Fuck. There was no way I was gonna get in there. I didn't know many seniors, and the ones I did were in my frat, so they wouldn't help. Late that night I stuffed Tagger under my frat jacket and walked over there anyway. I knew which window was Tyler's. He was on the end on the second floor overlooking the quad. When I got there, I could see his light was on. I stepped back to get the angle so I could see in, and there he was walking back and forth in his room. While I stood there in the dark on the quad, I saw Tyler throwing on a jacket. Then the light in his room went out. Fuck, was this my chance? Was he coming out?

I stood behind a tree and kept an eye on the front door of the dorm. Sure enough after a minute or two, there was Tyler walking out. He was crossing the quad and passed by the other side of the tree I hid behind. I had to channel some private detective shit and tail him. If I left enough distance between us, I would look like just another student walking, but if I let him get too far away, I might lose him.

I ducked from tree to tree across the quad. When he walked between two buildings on the other side, I sped up to keep him close. He went across a parking lot that was pretty empty, all the day commuter students off campus by this hour, but I ducked from one random, solitary car to the next. I wondered where he was going when he made his way out the back gate of campus.

Tyler was wearing a dark jacket and dark jeans, so it was hard to see him in the night. He walked down the sidewalk of the dark side street behind campus. I crossed to the other side and followed along. At the end of that street he walked into a wooded city park. It was a great park to hang in during the day. It was big with a lot of trails through the woods, some open fields where we played frisbee and touch football. But at night, I figured Tyler must be going for a walk. This was gonna be perfect. He's out for a quiet walk in the woods. I'll jump out and yell, 'Tagger! You're It!' Not even on campus, he won't expect it at all.

I sped up again to get to the entrance of the park before he disappeared from my view but not so close he would see me, and I just barely got a quick glimpse of Tyler disappearing into the wooded trail that looped all the way around the park. Fuck, how was I going to get away with stalking him without being seen?

I darted ahead to the start of the trail and saw him getting further into the trees ahead. I hid behind a tree for a second, then walked quickly ahead, then ducked behind another one. It was super dark now, late at night, in the middle of the trees, no park lights in this area. I tried to step quietly, but with leaves and sticks, I had to be super careful. And I lost him.

Fuck. Now there I was in the middle of a dark, wooded area of the park, with a teddy bear stuffed inside my frat jacket. I figured the path was one way through the trees, so I followed behind. I thought I could catch up to him and then just pounce and toss Tagger at him. My heart stopped when I saw a figure right near me behind a tree. Fuck, he was right there. But then I realized it wasn't Tyler. It was an older dude, really round, and just staring at me. What the fuck. I rolled my eyes and thought, this is fucking creepy. Was he a drug dealer? A thief? Was I about to get mugged?

Shit, what was I thinking being out here? I decided to push ahead and get this over with. I took a bunch of quick steps to avoid a knife to my throat. The path turned once or twice, and I got away from the weird stranger. That's when I heard some noise ahead. There was a bunch of trees all grown together in a group ahead of me, and I saw Tyler turn and disappear behind them. Got him!

I crept up to the trees and hid behind them. I heard sound on the other side, so I knew he was there. I peeked around really quickly, and I saw the back of him standing behind the trees. There were a few more sounds, so I knew he was still there. It was time to act and act fast. I pulled Tagger out of my jacket and held him in my hand.

I leapt out from my hiding spot behind the tree and jumped around to the other side. I was only two or three feet away when I got out just a quick blurted, "TAG..," but I stopped my call out when I realized the guy standing there wasn't Tyler. He turned his head quickly to me with a look of utter surprise on his face. It wasn't a student. This guy looked older, like maybe 30 or something.

There I was standing in the middle of the woods behind campus at night, holding a stuffed animal in the air pointed at a stranger. That's when I looked down and saw Tyler. He was on his knees in front of this guy. His hands were on the guy's hips, and he was sucking his dick. He pulled back and this big, long dick popped out of Tyler's mouth. It flopped in front of his face when he looked at me with sheer terror in his eyes. I didn't know what to do. I was frozen there. Tyler looked at me with that same terror in his eyes.

I turned heel and took off running. Oh shit. Oh shit. Now I knew what that old guy was doing behind the tree. Tyler was sucking that guy's cock. It's late at night. Damn, that was a nice-looking cock. I'm in the woods out here. Oh shit, people are gonna think I'm out here for this. Who was that old guy Tyler was with? Fuck, Tyler was sucking that dude. Tyler's gay. I have to get out of here. Damn, Tyler looked good there on his knees. Wait, what?

I ran full speed back down that side street. By the time I crossed through the back gate back onto campus, I was panting like crazy, sweating in my jacket. The thoughts were flooding through my mind. I tore my jacket off and put it under my arm. I had to catch my breath. If people see me, they'll wonder where I was, what got me so out of breath. That's when I realized, I no longer had Tagger. I must have dropped it in the woods.

I lay in bed that night looking up at the ceiling. My roommate was sound asleep, and I was alone with my thoughts. Damn, I had no idea Tyler was gay. Now he was probably afraid I was gonna tell everyone. I wasn't going to tell anyone, was I? How did I not know about that park at night? What was I gonna do about losing Tagger? Was it still out there in the woods? Will I have to admit I lost it? Why did I think Tyler looked so good while he was going down on that guy? Well, he did. He looked really good, the way his blond hair shone in the dark.

All night long I lay there on my bed not sleeping. One o'clock. Two o'clock. Three. Four. I just kept thinking about everything. Why did I love being in the frat so much? What was I going to do about that fucking stuffed animal? It was a long, long night. I don't know how much self-realization I had accomplished before that night. Maybe I'd been further along than I had even admitted to myself. But several things came into full bloom in my head. But the most important one was this: it wasn't just Tyler that was gay.

It was Thursday. The last day of Tag. And there would be a frat party tonight where the loser would be announced. Only problem was, Tagger was lost in the woods. If I was the one who lost him, it would come out. My three friends knew I was the one who had him last. They also knew our plan was to target Tyler. I didn't know what to do.

That's when the text messages started on our group thread.

Curtis. Well! Did you get him!

Scott. Is Tyler It?

Josh. Last day. Did you get rid of Tagger?

I didn't know what to say. That I lost it? What if it ended up getting found? I couldn't admit to anything until I found Tagger. I texted back, Wouldn't you like to know?

Josh. You still have it? Don't give it to me!

This might work out. They'll avoid me all day. After my first class, I decided I should go over to that park and see if I can find that damn bear. I didn't know then that those kind of places were only popular with guys late at night, so I worried on my way over. Would that dude still be behind the tree? Would there be guys there sucking dick? Would any of them be hot?

I walked that entire path. I was alone the entire time, not a single person was around. But neither was Tagger. So it was gone. I was going to have to fess up to losing it tonight. That would make me the big Loser and worse. I'd go down in history as the dude who lost Tagger.

Fuck my life. The rest of the day was a blur as I fretted about what they were going to do to me. Hell, running around in my underwear was fine. Even getting doused with beer or shit. But Tyler would be running the show. How would that go down? Maybe he wouldn't be so mean, knowing that I knew what he did. You know what? I realized. What was I worried about? I was the one who could tell everyone about him.

By the time the party was about to start, and the deadline for getting rid of Tagger came, I made my way over to the apartment three of my frat brothers shared where the party was going to start. I made sure to wear a good pair of underwear. I joined a few of my brothers, and they started relating stories about how the bear got passed around during the week. I was silent, but I was piecing together the travels of the bear up to the point where Curtis ended up with him on Wednesday morning. I looked around. He and Josh and Scott weren't there yet, so no one told the story of how it came to me.

I had just refilled my cup from the tap when I saw them come in all together. They looked over at me and pointed. Rushing over to me, Curtis whispered, "So did you get Tyler? Did you get him?"

Josh added, "Fuck you don't still have it, do you?"

I shrugged. Scott asked, "Then where is it?"

I finished pouring my beer. I was gonna have to admit to losing it in front of everyone soon. I wasn't going to enjoy this night. I grabbed three empty cups and gave them to my friends. I grabbed the tap and poured each of them a beer. I was trying to avoid their questions. They were happy the beer was flowing, but after I got one to each of them, and they had a taken a swig, Curtis looked back at me, "So?"

I cleared my throat and was about to tell them about losing Tagger when the front door opened, and everyone in the room started hooting. Skeet and another senior stepped in followed by Tyler. I looked over still worried about the whole situation, but all my thoughts blew up in my head. Tyler was walking into the room with a sheepish look on his face while he held Tagger in his hands over his head.

Everyone in the room started cheering or laughing as they realized our frat president was announcing that he himself was the final It. The cheers and laughter and cat-calling were ear-splitting. My three friends around me were all pounding on my back and screaming, "You did it! You did it!" People were hearing that, and word was spreading out of the kitchen.

"Bobby tagged Tyler!"

"Tyler is it!"

"The president is It? Holy shit!"

Tyler made his way to the center of the living room with Skeet and the other senior by his side. The other board members joined them. More people circulated around me to give me thumbs up or pat me. I looked over to the middle of the room. Tyler stood there with a smile on his face and was nodding his acceptance of his situation to people around him. "Yeah, it's me," he was saying. "I got Tagged."

Skeet silenced the crowd and announced, "So we have our Loser! And for the first time ever it's the prez! Ty-ler! Ty-ler!" He started repeating the name until everyone joined in chanting, Tyler Tyler Tyler. I even got caught up in it and called out his name. Skeet quieted everyone down again and said, "Why don't you tell us how you ended up our big Loser?"

Tyler pulled Tagger out from under his arm. His eyes surveyed the room until they fell on me. We stared at each other. I felt him looking at me. It felt like the first time ever. I grew warm. I could feel a flush on my face.

Tyler pointed the bear at me. "It was Bobby! He got me at the door to my dorm just as I walked outside." People were all turning to look at me. Tyler added in, "Right there on the quad!"

I smiled at all the faces looking at me. Then I looked back over at Tyler. He was still staring at me with a big smile on his face. Skeet urged me to come forward. I stepped through as everyone got out of my way. Skeet pulled me past the last few bodies and pushed me shoulder to shoulder against Tyler. I looked at him. He looked at me. He smiled wider and put his arm around my shoulder. "You got me fair and square, Bobbo!"

I felt his arm around me, his eyes on me, like I never had before. The memory of the first day I ever saw him came flashing back to my mind. He was behind a table on the quad, passing out flyers to freshmen trying to get them to pledge to the frat. We talked for like fifteen minutes about how awesome it was to be in a frat. You become brothers for life. You have each other's back. And you party.

Only now was I admitting to myself as I stood there in his arm. Tyler was the reason I joined. He was so hot. His big round eyes. The way he looked in his frat jacket. The way his hand touched mine when he handed me that flyer. The way he called me Bobbo. Those red lips. What they were doing in the park behind that tree.

All eyes were on us. Skeet called out to the room. "Now, usually our president would be in charge tonight. But since he can't be our leader tonight, we have to elect someone for the festivities. Now who should it be?"

The room started calling out names. Skeet! Curtis! But then Bobby! And more and more people landed on my name. Bobby! Until the room was chanting again. This time instead of Tyler, it was Bobby! Bobby! Bobby!

Skeet announced, "OK! For tonight and tonight only, Tyler, you are not our president! You are our Loser! And you'll do whatever we say!" Cheers erupted. Skeet leaned into my ear, "We've got some games already planned, so I will let you know what to make him do."

I turned away from Tyler and looked at Skeet. "OK."

"You know how we do it. Embarrass him. He'll do whatever you say." Skeet looked right at me with this big stupid grin on his face. "Right, Tyler? You have to do whatever Bobby wants!" Cheers erupted.

I turned back to Tyler. With all the noise around us, no one heard him but me. He looked me in the eyes as he pulled his arm away from around my shoulder. He was still looking me right in the eyes when a sad look washed over him. His whisper sounded pleading. "I'll do whatever you say."

I knew what he meant. He didn't want me to tell anyone about him. Skeet was already handing out markers to a bunch of guys. No one noticed how Tyler and I just stood there next to each other, the sense of tension between us only felt by us. I looked him in those eyes. "I would never tell," I said.

He nodded. I felt his hand grab mine and squeeze. He looked so relieved. He smiled. Then he announced to the room. "Bobbo! I will do whatever you say!"

Everyone in the room screamed out at once the second I shouted right into Tyler's face, "Strip!"

He immediately bent down and pulled his pants down. He got them over his sneakers, and as he pulled his shirt off over his head, he jumped up on the couch to show the room that he was wearing nothing but a jockstrap.

The festivities commenced. While Skeet had announced that Tyler would do whatever I said, it was him who fed into my ear what to make him do. They had already planned out the night's embarrassing escapades. First Skeet leaned into my ear and made me order Tyler to the middle of the room where a bunch of people surrounded him. They drew all over his body with markers. Cat whiskers. Handprints on his exposed butt cheeks. Arrows across his stomach pointing at his jock. How had I never gotten such a good look at that stomach? The slight amount of soft brown fuzz down the middle. I grabbed a marker and drew concentric circles around both of his nipples. I looked up. He was smiling at me. How did I never touch that chest before? I felt dizzy.

Someone started spinning him in a circle as they held markers to him, covering him in lines. First he was facing me with that beautiful chest, those lips, those eyes. Then he was spun around, and I saw that sweet little ass out for everyone to see. Then his face again, that body, that bulge inside his jockstrap. His ass again. Face. Ass. Chest. Bulge. I couldn't stop looking at him. I was soaking in every inch of him.

We led him outside. He was pushed forward, and we all flooded out of the apartment and crossed the street back to campus. Good thing there were no cops around. Once on campus, Tyler in just a jockstrap led a parade of our entire fraternity and our sister sorority and all our party guests. We led him through the quad. He had a grin on his face the entire time.

In front of the freshmen dorm, Skeet told me to order him to the wall. He stood there. Above him there were a bunch of faces at every window. They opened each of them, second floor, third floor, fourth. First a red plastic cup appeared out of one of the windows. It was turned upside down, and beer poured down over Tyler's head. Cheers erupted.

The beer was followed by another one and another. Then someone held out a giant cooler, and we watched as a huge amount of water splashed down on his head. It must have been ice cold, because I heard Tyler shriek then pull his arms around himself and crouch down.

Next it was off to this steep expanse of lawn behind the student center. In the winter, we would sled down it on cafeteria trays. Now in the springtime, Tyler was led to the top of the hill and ordered to roll down. He looked hysterical in nothing but his jockstrap, his bright white butt shining in the evening darkness.

He came back up to the top, and we could see he was covered in grass clippings. The sticky beer acted like glue, and he was a total mess. Next Skeet made me announce that we were ordering him out to the athletic field. When we got there, I noticed the sprinklers were on. It looked like they'd been on for a while, because the field was soaked with puddles everywhere. Someone must have had a friend in maintenance, because this was definitely planned.

Three seniors picked Tyler up and brought him to the middle of the field. They found the biggest puddle and put him down in the middle of it and started rolling him around. The mud started kicking up. Not just Tyler, but the three of them all became a muddy mess. People joined in. It was a mud fest. Everyone rolled around in the mud. Tyler was always in the middle of it, but now everyone was involved.

We were all laughing and having the most amazing time ever. Curtis and Scott got into it and were wrestling around in the mud. Josh found me and hit me in the chest with a handful of mud. We were raging and screaming. It probably was not the best idea in the world, because no one was going to go back to the apartment now and continue the party, which should have gone all night long. Little by little people extricated themselves and headed back to the dorms to shower.

I found I was one of the last ones there. Having led the festivities, I stayed the longest. Before I knew it, it was just a small crew of us. Skeet and a few other seniors. Curtis, Scott, Josh, and I. And there in the middle of us was Tyler. Covered in mud. Still wearing just a jockstrap.

I went over to him. He was lying in the mud, laughing with a big smile on his face. I stood over him. he looked up from where he lay at my feet. I reached a hand down to help him up. He grabbed it, but instead of standing up, he pulled me down. I fell by his side in the mud. I had to laugh.

Lying there beside him, both of us absolutely filthy, I looked into his eyes but couldn't find any words. He looked back at me. The smile left his face, and he said simply, "Thank you."

I still couldn't find the words. I just nodded my head. Clueless and speechless, my hand still in his, I turned it around into the frat's handshake. He returned it with a shake and let out a sigh. I could not wrap my head around what I wanted to do right there. So I stood up, turned away, and walked back to my room.

I could not sleep. Again. That night I found myself lying in bed again staring at the ceiling. My roommate was sound asleep. I could hear him breathing slowly. My mind was going in circles, making loops, avoiding some thoughts, landing on others. Things at long last were making sense to me. Things were all fucked up, and nothing seemed right. My life made sense and confused me all at once.

But there was one thing I could not stop thinking about. In and out of my head, there was Tyler. The day we met. Being accepted a few months later. Tyler congratulating me and calling me Bobbo for the first time. How did it happen that it was Tyler now that was the reason why nothing made sense in my head? How could it possibly be that it was Tyler of all people that was behind that tree? How could it be that Tyler was... like me?

I couldn't sleep. I couldn't stay there. I had to walk. I put on a pair of sweats, my sneaks, a t-shirt. I walked out onto campus. I told myself I was just walking, but my mind and my feet conspired, and they walked with purpose in a straight line. And I found myself outside the senior dorm, looking up at a window. It was late, really late. I saw a light on.

I walked straight to the front door. I didn't know how I was going to get in. I just walked in. There at the front desk was a security guard. He was sound asleep. I walked right past to the stairwell. One door opened. I climbed a flight of stairs. Another door opened. And I was on the second floor.

I walked to the end to the door I knew was the one I wanted. I stood there in front of it. I breathed in. I breathed out. I closed my eyes and opened them again. And I knocked.

The door opened, and there he was standing in front of me. Tyler. He had showered and cleaned up in the hours since I last saw him lying on the ground. In the mud. In his jockstrap. He stared at me. I stared at him. He stepped back. I stepped in.

Tyler shut the door and stood there next to it and next to me. "Bobbo," he said my name.

I turned to him. "You're still It."

He looked at me confused. "What?"

I let out every breath in my lungs and all my hesitancy with it. "You're still It. You ended up with the bear."

He just looked at me. "Yeah," he said. "You dropped it. I picked it up."

I looked into his eyes. I looked deep into his eyes. I knew what I wanted. "You have to do what I say," I said.

Tyler's eyes went wide. I could tell he didn't know what to say. I said what I had come to say to him. "Show me what you were doing behind that tree." I reached over and locked the door.

He looked at me, for one moment confused. "Are you sure?"

I stepped closer. I leaned in so our lips touched. Electricity coursed through my entire body. This was everything I'd ever wanted. "Please."

Tyler's hands were on me. They started by reaching up and touching my chest. He ran them down my body to the top of my sweatpants. He pulled, and as they got loose, they pulled away from my body. I remembered I hadn't put anything on underneath. They were around my ankles in a second. Tyler's hand was around my cock. He leaned in and kissed my lips more fully. His tongue darted into my mouth. I touched it with mine. I put my hand on the back of his neck and pulled tight, planting the kiss on him hard. I loosened my grip, and he slid down slowly. Little bit by little bit, he lowered himself, his lips closer and closer to where I wanted them to be.

His hand gripped around the base of my cock that by this point was so hard it was almost sore. Tyler's lips were on it. I looked down and watched the head disappear into his mouth. As I felt the moist warmth sliding over me, down all the way down to the bottom of my shaft, I sighed heavily. Tyler buried my entire cock down his throat. He paused and held it there before sliding off of it. He held just the head in again and looked up at me before sliding all the way down on it again.

I watched him. He watched me. Those beautiful lips were stretched and wrapped around my cock. A half smile was on his lips as he went down on me again and again and again. Yes, this is exactly what I had always wanted. This and more. I wanted him to do this again and again and again. I wanted to do it to him. I wanted to see his ass in that jockstrap again. I wanted to fuck that ass. I wanted to touch every square inch of his body. I wanted to taste him. I wanted to be with him. But right there in that moment, I wanted him to suck my cock and love it. I wanted to hear him moan with pleasure. I had heard that sound in the woods. That sound he was making right before he saw me. I needed to hear it.

And then I did. I heard it. He moaned with a pleasure I knew I could never live without. My cock down his throat. His hand wrapped around me and resting on my ass. And Tyler made that sound. He made it for me that time. I looked into his eyes. He looked into mine. And he made that sound again. That sweet, long mmmm sound. And I lost control. My entire body was washed over with desire. I breathed in and out fast and hard. My balls quivered, my cock thrust out even harder, and I shot wet and hard.

Tyler then made another sound. A sound of surprise and of excitement. He bobbed his head vigorously up and down my shaft. I could feel the hot liquid slick in his mouth, on his lips, as he slid on and off of my cock. My balls were in his hand when he finally let it fall from his lips. Rising he looked me in the eyes, an expectant smile on his lips. I planted a hard kiss on his lips. I opened his mouth with my tongue and kissed him passionately. My arms wrapped around him. He was still fully clothed. That had to change. I still wore a t-shirt, my sweatpants crammed down around my ankles.

"I'm sorry," I said.

He looked at me confused. "Sorry?"

"Not sorry. I mean, I didn't want you to think I just wanted... you know, to make you do that."

He smiled at me, a wide smile. It melted my heart, he was so hot. "You didn't make me do that, Bobbo. I wanted to. I've always wanted to. I just can't believe you saw me in the park like that. That's not me."

I didn't let go of him, my arms still wrapped around him. "I didn't know you..," I trailed off, but he answered.

"I didn't know you either," he said. My sentence was interrupted, but his sounded complete.

"I didn't know me either," I replied.

He grabbed me tighter. "Well, hello then."

"Hello."

"So," he asked. "Is that all?"

"What do you mean?"

Tyler looked me in the eyes. Then he pulled his face next to mine. His cheek against mine, his lips brushed up against my ear. "Well, I still have to do what you say."

All these years later, some nights he still rolls over and whispers that into my ear, and I smile.

The Frat Boy in Make-Up

by Matthew Cooper

Like most college theater programs, we had our share of gay guys. There were four of us that regularly tried out for student productions. Usually we'd all end up getting cast, even if it was for crappy small parts with no lines. The director was one of the professors from our Speech and Theatre department. Professor Spencer Lancaster. He liked it when we called him Spence. He always said, "There are no small parts, only small actors." Well, there was one play where I had one line and appeared on stage once. No small parts, my ass.

So the four of us were the best of friends, and yeah, at one cast party or another, I ended up at least making out with one of my three closest friends. Jay was a cute, short blond a year older than me. When I tried out for the first play of my freshman year, he invited me back to his dorm room, and we ended up sucking each other off. He had a really nice pink dick, but it didn't go any further than that one time. We ended up the best of friends, and I always joke that he corrupted me. Not true, but it was always funny.

Arthur was the same year as I was, but he didn't try out for the fall productions. We met him in the spring of my freshman year. Jay and I were both in a production of A Midsummer Night's Dream as Rude Mechanicals. Not many lines, but our scenes were great comedic relief from the whiny lovers. Arthur had tried out but didn't get cast. We introduced ourselves standing in front of the casting sheet when it was posted on the department bulletin board. He was looking sad and dejected, so we took him under our wing and urged him to keep trying. OK, so it was because he was so damn cute with his puppy dog eyes looking all sad and his runner's body with slim, little waist.

Peter got cast in the last show of the year, and I got a pretty good handjob backstage during the final dress rehearsal.

Then the first show of Arthur's and my sophomore year, when Jay was a junior, we all placed bets on whether this new freshman Peter was on our team or not. He was cute with dark hair, clearly worked out, scruff on his face, pouty lips. He was definitely passable as a straight guy, but he'd looked me in the eyes for a few seconds too long.

So I said yes he definitely was. Jay and Arthur said no. And I won the bet. I also ended up rolling around naked with Peter in his apartment off campus a few weeks later. Both of us grinding our cocks against each other for like half an hour, kissing and groping each other, before he finally asked me, "So do you want to fuck me?"

I laughed and said, "I was going to ask you the same thing." So yeah, nothing more happened there.

But I also found out that Jay had already beaten me to it by blowing him a few days before that. He did the same thing he had done with me—an innocent sounding invite to hang in his dorm room that ended in a mutual suck fest. So predictable.

So yeah, four gay guys all together, best of friends, and not a top among us. After Peter and I realized in our failed attempt at a hot and steamy escapade in his room, we grilled Arthur a few days later about what kind of guy he likes, and he admitted he was a total bottom.

You have got to laugh; otherwise, you would cry. Four horny young college boys with pretty decent cocks—if I do say so myself—all friends, all out to each other, but it just did not work between us. While every now and then we'd end up blowing each other or just cuddling in one of our beds, we all wanted the same thing. We were four bottoms in search of a top.

Jay was our unappointed leader. Mostly because he was the oldest and usually got better parts than the rest of us. But also because he was such a little slut with a dirty mouth who loved to tell us all about his latest sexcapade. Whether it was a late-night blowjob in his dorm room—he was nothing if not consistent—or an online hookup with some random local living in town, or the holy grail of gay college fantasies—a drunk frat boy in the middle of the night who figured a mouth is a mouth, Jay loved to tell us about every little detail.

Since Peter had his own apartment, thank you Mommy the anesthesiologist, we usually would hang out in his living room. We'd drink cheap beer, play videogames, troll the online apps, all of us looking for the same damn thing, and Jay would start telling us about his latest conquest. He would play this game where he made us admit when his story made us hard. It was the craziest thing to do being just friends and all, but we were all admitted horn dogs, and hey, we'd all fooled around with each other at least a little. So Jay would tell his story, and we would see who could hold out the longest without getting hard. Jay would force us to outline our cocks through our shorts or jeans when we got hard. Last one standing would have to outline his to prove he wasn't. How it never ended in a hot foursome orgy on the floor of Pete's living room, I'll never know. Probably because we all knew it would be futile.

If only I could have made myself into a top, I would have all three of them to fuck whenever I wanted. But I'm that most extreme case of total bottom. I am a proud, card-carrying, Size Queen. And my friends all knew it. I always lost Jay's game if he started telling us how big the cock of the guy he had hooked up with was.

I dreamed of big, giant cocks. I wanted to see big, thick, fat, juicy cock. I didn't care if it was cut or uncut, curved or straight. My search engine knew what I wanted. 'Big cock.' 'Giant penis.' 'Huge dick.' And my friends knew it, too. Jay the cocksucker. Arthur who fantasized about threesomes. Peter who loved big meatheads and jocks. And me, oh I'm Eric, by the way, Eric the Size Queen.

There we were, second semester of my sophomore year. Audition notice went up for some original play the chairman of the department had written. I don't even remember the name of it, but trust me, you've never heard of it. It was terrible. I'm pretty sure that is the one and only time it was ever put on a stage.

The four of us showed up to the audition. Spence was directing again. He was there and so was the department chairman. That guy wasn't going to trust anyone with his baby. He whispered into Spence's ear the entire time we sat there waiting for our turn to audition. After each student went up and read, he practically chewed on the director's ear.

Peter went up to read, and Spence told him to read for the part of Jake. He told him Jake was a washed up boxer who was too old to compete, still in peak shape, but couldn't deal with getting old. Jay, Arthur, and I listened to Pete's monologue and thought he was awesome. Now the thing about college theater is, you have these parts that are meant to be people of all sorts of ages, but every single one of the actors is between 18 and 21. What are you gonna do?

After Peter sat down, Professor Lancaster whispered to the chairman. The chairman whispered back. Spence answered back more audibly, "They're all the same age. We're not going to find someone who looks like an older adult." That's when the chairman got too loud, and I'm sure he regrets it, but we all heard him snap back, "But they all sound so queer. This guy is a boxer. He's a stud."

Spence looked super pissed off, but this was his boss. Probably to avoid any further insult or potential lawsuits, he asked us all to clear the room. But our interest was way too peaked, and frankly, we were way too offended to go far, so we eavesdropped from backstage as the chairman ranted about our abilities as actors, and our director—bless his heart—defended us and stood up for the whole bunch of students who auditioned. "These kids put their hearts into this program. They're here for every show. You can't just toss them aside."

It went on like that for a while until the chairman stormed out with a final, "At least find one guy who can play the boxer!"

Spence called us back in. The four of us were in a cluster behind a bunch of the other theater kids. He came over to us directly and stopped us on our way back to the audience seats. He put a hand on my shoulder and motioned for the four of us to stop. "I'm really sorry you had to hear that, you guys. That was uncalled for."

We shrugged it off and told him not to worry about it. We'd heard worse, and it meant a lot to have him call it out. Assholes, what are you gonna do, am I right?

Spence finished the auditions, thanked us, and we all went off to wait the day or so until the casting sheet went up to see if we got parts. Despite the chairman's outburst and what we were hearing about how bad the play was, we were all student actors, we had our egos, and we all wanted parts no matter what.

The next day I walked by the department bulletin board at least ten times. Nothing. The next day Jay and I walked by together in the morning on our way to class. Nothing. At lunchtime all four of us were eating in the cafeteria and decided to go again and check. Still no casting sheet. Arthur admitted he checked several times that day. So did Peter. OK, I may have walked over after dinner. The sheet was almost always up the very next day.

Finally, on the third day, I woke up in my dorm room and had almost forgotten about it when my phone dinged. There was a group text message from Jay to all of us. It's up! I texted back, OMG don't tell me. Meet U guys there.

We were theater geeks. OK, theater queens. And this was like our Oscar nominations day. Who got a part? Who was gonna have to volunteer to be a stage manager or props manager if they still wanted to be part of the show? Who got a lead?

I practically ran across campus to the Humanities building. As I got close, I saw Arthur up ahead of me and called out to him to wait up for me. We got to the front door when Peter texted, wait for me outside we'll go up together.

Arthur and I stood by the front door of the building when Jay texted back, too late already here. Arthur and I shrugged and went up. Jay was standing at the board along with a few girls who were squawking happily because they both got parts.

By the time we got to the board, Peter came running up from behind. "Thanks for waiting," he said through heavy breaths. He'd clearly run clear across campus. But that's when I looked at Jay's face. He had a smile, but as soon as he looked at me, he stopped and tilted his head.

I saw the column of character names on the left but ignored it. The column that mattered was our names. I saw Jay's name pretty high up on the list. "Jay! You got a lead! That's awesome." He didn't say anything.

I scrolled my finger down. About halfway down, there was Arthur's name. I didn't remember his character name from auditions. "Hey, Arthur. Check it out."

"Who is Mr. Stanford," he asked. "I don't remember reading for that part."

Peter blurted out from behind me, "Hey! That's me! I got a part!"

I moved my finger down and saw his name next to his part. "Congrats," I said.

"Townsperson #3? What the fuck."

I turned around to look at him and smiled, "Remember, there are no small parts..."

Jay and Arthur finished the saying, "Just small actors."

That's when I realized my finger had reached the bottom of the list. My three friends had suddenly gotten really quiet. "Oh," I said.

Jay put his hand on my shoulder, "Sorry, buddy."

Peter then asked, "Hey who got that part of the boxer? I thought I had a shot."

Arthur nudged closer to the list. "Who's Jack Rendall?"

The suckiest part of being part of the theater program was having to audition for every show and the fear of not getting cast. All three of my friends were going to be busy with rehearsals several nights a week and running lines. I was going to be facing more than a month alone in my room with my posse all part of something without me. I didn't want to be left out, so I volunteered to be the props manager. When I went to Spence's office, he apologized that I didn't get a part but asked me to be at all the rehearsals so I could note what we would need for the production.

There I was sitting in the audience seats with my boys on a Tuesday night. The other cast members trickled in with their scripts in hand. I just had a yellow legal pad and a pen. We waved over at our friend Janice who got the female lead. She was sitting with a few other girls.

Professor Lancaster came in and asked everyone to sit down. "I see almost everyone is here, so while we wait for the rest, let's get started." He nodded at me and asked the actors for the first scene to get up on stage and start a read-through.

That's when the loudest crashing sound rang out as someone pulled on the side doors at the top of the house that everyone who was part of the theater knew were always chained shut. The chains rattled loudly, and it echoed through the room. Whoever it was pulled a second time, and again the whole room was filled with the sound of metal banging on glass.

Jay rolled his eyes and called out, "Other door!" Several of the student actors were grimacing or making frustrated grunting sounds. Then the main door swung open, and in walked a stranger. As he got closer, my eyes bulged wide open. I couldn't turn away, but I'm sure the six eyes of my friends reacted similarly. Walking down the center aisle of the auditorium was a fucking stud. The kind of stud you never ever ever see in a college theater.

My eyes took him in, and time stood still as he came closer and closer. Red hair. The hottest turned up nose I've ever seen. Two lips that were more like pillows. His body seemed big, but it was covered in a varsity jacket with Greek letters on it. His hands were in the pockets of his jeans, which seemed to cover tree trunks instead of legs. In between the open front of that jacket, I could see a white t-shirt straining in the middle of a well-rounded chest.

He got closer, and when he was near the end of the row the four of us were sitting in, he turned in behind us and sat in the next row a few seats down near the aisle. I turned back around and looked at Peter to my right. "Close your mouth, whore," I had to say to him. He looked at me, his eyes were clearly as wide as mine were.

Arthur nudged my left side and had a grin on his face. Jay on the other side of Peter mumbled probably a little too loud, "Who is he!"

I looked down at my legal pad. Arthur's hand was crushing my thigh. Peter and Jay were giggling. I looked over at Janice and the girls. They were all whispering to each other and throwing looks over their shoulders.

Spence realized there was a commotion and turned to see the newcomer. "Ah, welcome. Everyone, this is Jack. He is our boxer." That explained it. Jack Rendall. This was going to be fun. "Now guys, Jack has never been in a show before, so please welcome him, be nice, and help him out."

What I was able to piece together from various rumors, the department chairman and Spence had a raging fight for a few days over casting. The department chair threatened to pull the play. Spence told him if he was going to be so stubborn over who played his boxer, then he should go out and find someone. And so he did. Jack Rendall, a frat boy who had never been in a show before, not even in high school. I guess he offered him extra credit in a class he was no doubt failing or something.

Rehearsals went as well as could be expected with what turned out to be a pretty stupid script. I was busy taking notes on set dressings and props then searching stuff out from the old props room. It was boring, but I didn't mind, because it meant I could be at every rehearsal even if I really didn't have to be, and no one would question it. And I would go pretty much unnoticed, so I could just sit there and stare at Jack Rendall.

Of course, after that first night, the jacket came off, and there he was in just his t-shirt. His chest, his arms, shoulders. He was a fucking stud. His thighs were so thick, he looked like a soccer player or something. But trust me, if you know anything about frat boys, they're not jocks or athletic. They don't go in for things like theater. They pretty much just go to the gym to get built up, and they drink and act obnoxious. But Jack didn't seem to be any of those things. He was super quiet, learned his lines, and sat watching when he wasn't in a scene.

The girls all hit on him. He loved the attention. He probably banged half of them within the first week or so of rehearsals. One Thursday night, Janice was putting the moves on him. I was sitting close by, and if he didn't realize he could have her any time he wanted, he must be stupid as fuck. But he smiled at her, answered her questions, and she rolled her hair in her fingers and laughed too much. Finally she said, "So hey, the whole cast is gonna go for drinks after rehearsal. You wanna join us?"

He paused, probably a little bit too long for her, so she added, "It's OK if you have something else to do, you know a frat party or something."

That got him. "No, no, it's cool." He rose up out of the slouch he was always in. 'Yeah, that's cool. It'd be good, you know, to get to know everybody."

I don't know how I got the nerve, but I interrupted them with a plan. "So hey, Janice, if we don't have anywhere else to go, we could all go hang at Peter's apartment."

Janice looked over at me. At first, I think she thought I was trying to cock-block her, but then I guess she thought it would give her a chance at Jack. "Yeah, totally," she sing-songed. "A good old fashioned cast party." She turned back to Jack and put her hand on his shoulder. I think she left it there a little too long if you ask me. And she said to him, "And you'll come."

He nodded at her and looked at me. "Yeah, sure. Thanks."

I smiled at him and died a little on the inside. "Great. We'll go pick up booze. Jan, can you show him where it is?"

She gave me a big smile. "Yeah." She turned back to him. 'You can come with me."

Then all I had to do was tell Peter he was hosting a party. At first he got pissed, but then I told him Jack was coming. That got him.

It had seemed like a good idea when I first blurted it out at rehearsal, and it was funny for sure. We were all tipsy and dancing and having a great time. But there was no pulling Janice off of Jack. All the four of us got was more staring at him from across the room for most of the night.

And Jack was loving the attention. If her hand wasn't on his shoulder, his was around her waist. They danced in the living room, went to the kitchen to get more beers together. I swear if he had to pee, she'd probably try to go with him. Actually, thinking about it, she might have done just that. The only upside was getting to watch him dance in that flimsy t-shirt, getting a look at his firm body as he wrapped his arms around someone, even if it wasn't me. And after a while, he started to sweat, and the way his hair stuck to his forehead, I don't know, I think if we were playing Jay's sex-story game, I would have lost, because I swear I was starting to get hard.

The night wore on into the early morning hours. You know how college parties are. We kept it going and going. Nobody ever registers for early classes on Fridays, so Thursday was a party night. But just in case neighbors complained, we turned the music down and all started lounging in the living room. People started making fun of the crappy show we were in and the cheesy dialogue.

Janice got up and performed one of her more pathetic monologues, and we all laughed as she overacted every emotion. She threw her hand over her forehead when she was supposed to be distraught, and flung herself onto the floor then across Jack's feet who sat on the couch. After the laughter subsided, Peter drew up enough nerve and asked a little too loudly, "So Jack, what do you think of acting?"

Everyone in the room got quiet and turned to the poor guy. I'm sure he could tell he was on the spot. I mean, we all knew each other. He was the new guy. Janice looked up at him from the floor by his feet. He kinda hemmed and hawed before answering, "It's cool I guess. I mean, for you guys this is all probably normal stuff and all, but learning all those lines and where to stand and all, it's all pretty new to me."

Janice patted his knee and said, "Oh you're doing fine. I'll help you run lines if you want." Damn, that's what I wanted to say.

"I mean, to be honest, my brothers are really razzing me about it. You know, being in a show."

Poor Janice, she asked, "Oh you have brothers?"

Jay and Arthur laughed the loudest. "My frat brothers, I mean. They think it's, I don't know, kinda..."

Janice blurted out, "Faggy?"

Jack looked like he was going to puke. Jay wasn't having it. "Bitch, what?"

Janice looked sheepishly over at him. "You know I didn't mean..."

Jack interrupted her though, "No, I mean, well, yeah. But come on, you know frat guys. They're not all that, you know, accepting."

"Yeah," Jay said. "But you're not like that, right?"

Jack couldn't have answered faster, "NO! I mean, it's.. I don't have any problem. I didn't mean..."

Jay put a pin in the tension. "It's OK. No offense."

The topic quickly changed. Nobody wanted to offend, I could tell Jack didn't mean to either. Or maybe I was just so enamored of him, he could have said anything, and I'd forgive him. But we were all friends, and Jack seemed cool so far, so we just went back to joking about the show and drinking.

I went to grab another beer in the kitchen, and as I closed the refrigeration, Jack was there with me, alone in Peter's little kitchen. My heart skipped a beat, but I was able to ask, "Need another beer?"

"Yeah," he answered. As I retrieved it and handed it to him, he added, "So hey, I didn't offend anybody, did I? I mean, that's not what I meant."

I nodded and waved my hand at him, "Nah, it's cool. Janice said it, not you, and she's drunk."

He snickered and raised his beer bottle to me. I clicked mine against his and said, "Cheers."

He didn't make a move to leave the kitchen, so of course, my feet didn't move.

He seemed like he wanted to say something, so I let the silence lie between us hoping he would. Finally, he asked, "So, am I the only straight guy here?"

I laughed. He looked me in the eyes, kinda embarrassed. But I had to think about who was still at the party. "No," I finally said. "Well, I mean, you're definitely in the minority."

He looked at me and stuttered, "But you are, right? Gay, I mean?"

My stomach lurched. "Yeah."

He looked at his feet. "Yeah, I figured. And Jay, of course." Oh, wait until I tell him Jack said, of course.

I nodded but added, "Why? Does that make you uncomfortable?"

He shrugged and tilted his beer back to me. I clinked it again. "Nah, it's cool." I wish I could have thought of something more to say to him, but he turned and went back out to the party. I watched his wide shoulders as he went out through the door. God, he was built.

I lingered in the kitchen for a few minutes. Jay, Arthur, and Peter all made their way in, and we whispered about Jack, his eyes, his chest, his arms, his legs. I swear, we were like stupid, little school girls. There was nothing to gain from it, so we dug into the cupboards for snacks. They got fresh beers, and we hung in the kitchen for a few minutes. Then we heard the music start back up, and a few girls were hooting in the living room. Oh, drunk, straight girls.

It seemed like the party was starting back up again. Peter probably worried about his neighbors complaining, but hey, it's not a party until it's gotten its second wind. That's when we heard Janice cackle, "Woo hoo! Take it off." All four of us bolted toward the door into the living room at the same time. All four of us landed in the doorway at the same time trying to push through.

When we finally did, there was Janice dancing on the couch. Three other girls were in the middle of the room. A few guys were there, too. And in the middle of it Jack was gyrating in some frat boy form of dancing. Shirtless. He had stripped his shirt off, and he was swinging it in an arc over his head. One of the other guys was pulling his off. I didn't care. Janice peeled her blouse over her head and was now dancing on the couch in her bra. But my eyes did not leave Jack.

Jack's chest was unbelievable. The two rounded muscular orbs of his pecs were on vivid display. his tiny little dark nipples looked out on the room like a pair of eyes. This frat boy had a washboard that led from that amazing chest down to his low-rise jeans. His skin was smooth—completely hairless except the faintest little wisp of a line of auburn that pointed down from his belly button to the top of those jeans. He had a huge smile on his face, and as he spun to face us, he called out, "Come on! Everybody dance!"

Who was I to say no? And my three buddies were not going to say no. We swung out in two pairs around both ends of the couch and joined the crazy straights in the middle of Peter's living room. I turned to smile at Jay who looked at me with a giant grin and shrugged. That's when I felt two hands on my sides grab me from behind. Jay almost spit up his beer. Those two hands grabbed the bottom of my t-shirt and pulled it up. I almost dropped my beer as they pulled it over my head.

I half-twisted and found Jack grabbing onto me by the shirt that was now pulled to my neck. He leaned into me and shouted, "Come on! Shirts off!" He managed it over my head. I moved my beer from one hand to the other while he wrangled it off of me and threw it across the room.

Janice was whooping louder than ever. I just smiled at Jack with a happy shock. He patted the middle of my chest and danced around me and grabbed at Jay. "Your turn," he called out before grabbing Jay's shirt just like he did mine and pulled it over his head. This time Jack grabbed the beer out of Jay's hand before pulling the shirt up over his head. Poor little Jay didn't reach much higher than Jack's chest. He got stuck with his arms still in the shirt over his head. When he pulled and pulled again, Jack noticed he was stuck, so he wrapped his arms all the way around Jay and picked him up off the floor and danced around with him, Jay's arms still up in the air. When he finally got his arms free, he found himself in a bear hug with the hunky frat boy who kissed the top of his head with a big grin before putting him down. I saw him lean into Jay's ear and say something. Jay turned to me and was blushing beat red like only a blond boy can.

Peter and Arthur missed their chance at a good groping but pulled their own shirts off themselves. While they were still on the other side of the little cluster of writhing bodies, Jay leaned up against me and put his hands around my shoulders. He gyrated against me and pressed his crotch against me to make me feel it. "I lose," he said. "I'm already hard."

I laughed and put my mouth against his ear, "What did he say to you?"

Jay answered, "He said, I never meant to offend you."

I danced away from Jay, and we just looked at each other. We were more in love with our big, straight frat boy than ever. He left with Janice.

A week before opening night, the costumes came in, and Spence started talking to everyone about their personal props, which I supplied, and their costumes, and their make-up. Jack was sitting near me, and he whispered to me, "We have to wear make-up?"

I said, "Well, yeah, you're supposed to be an aging boxer. You can't look like a frat boy." He looked surprised and maybe a little frightened. I said, "It's OK. Janice can help you, or any of the girls."

"I've never worn make-up before," he said.

"It's not like women's make-up. It's like part of your costume to make you look the part."

"Like what," he asked.

"Like you'll probably want to use gray hairspray to look old and draw in wrinkles around your eyes."

He look even more concerned. "I don't know how to do any of that."

I tried to reassure him. "The director will get you help."

He looked over at me. "Can you help me?"

I didn't expect that. "Sure."

Spence made actors treat the final dress rehearsal like it was opening night. It was a Wednesday night. The show would run two weekends with shows on Thursday, Friday, and Saturday nights. That Tuesday night as we finished rehearsal, Spence as usual announced that everyone should be at the theater an hour and a half before curtain to get into costumes and make-up, but then he called out, "Now Jack, you're gonna have more make-up than everyone else. You have to look much older. Gray hair, wrinkles. You think two hours is enough?"

Jack looked like he'd just realized he forgot his homework or someone told him his puppy had died. He stuttered back at Spence and blushed, "Um, I've never put make-up on before."

"Fine," Spence said. "You'll come early. Do I need to get you help?"

Jack immediately spoke up, "Eric is going to help me."

I got a knee in my right thigh from Jay and an elbow in my left side from Arthur. Jack turned around and smiled at me, and I got another double nudge from my friends before Spence announced, "OK, everyone get here at 6:30. At the latest, people." And then he added, "Jack and Erik, 5:30."

I thought of nothing else that entire day except the one full hour I was going to have with Jack. All alone, helping him put on his make-up. I fantasized about it. I worried about it. I avoided my friends all day so they wouldn't joke about it. I ended up skipping dinner and getting to the theater a full half-hour before that.

I turned on the backstage lights, opened the men's dressing room and checked inside to make sure the make-up was there. Someone had gone to the theater supply company, and there were several packed bags full of new cakes of foundation, pencils, and the gray hairspray Jack was going to need.

I realized there were no sponges or brushes and hoped they were in the women's dressing room. With a bit of concern, I pulled the door open to head over to check, but as I pulled it open and charged through, there was Jack standing in the way. I almost barreled right into him. "Oh," I said with a gasp. "You're early."

He had his hands in his pockets and looked downright scared. "Yeah, I'm just really nervous. You know, about this whole make-up thing. Am I gonna look stupid?"

I rolled my eyes at him and smiled. "Relax, no. It's to make you look the part, not like a girl. Think of it as special effects, not cosmetics."

He shrugged, "Yeah, OK. You're right. It's just if my friends come to the show, I'll never hear the end of it."

I'd done so many shows through high school and my first two years at college, I was more than familiar with this reaction. I reassured him, "Trust me. It'll be fine. Why don't you go in and get ready? I have to go find some sponges and brushes in the girls."

He nodded acceptance, and I moved to give him access to the door. Without thinking about it, before I left him, I said, "Oh, take your shirt off. You don't want to get make-up on it." And as I turned and ran down the hallway to the women's dressing room, what I had said dawned on me. Oh fuck yes, I was going to be getting really close to Jack. And he would be shirtless. By the time I went through the brushes and sponges and separated them equally for the two dressing rooms, I realized I was half hard with anticipation.

When I pulled the door open and stepped back into the men's, I lost my breath. Jack stood there in the middle of the room just pulling his pants off his feet. He had his costume pants on the back of the chair. His shirt was already hanging up, and he stood there in just his underwear. He had on cheap supermarket tighty-whities. Typical straight boy, Mom probably bought them for him. On anybody else, they would be the most unflattering thing you can imagine, but on Jack's rock hard body, it didn't matter.

His skin was smooth and looked like milk. His chest that I was seeing for the second time took my breath away. Did he live in the gym? As he was bent over pulling off his pants, I saw his round, muscular ass. His arms were flexing a bit as he pulled a pant leg over his socked feet.

I didn't speak. I couldn't. I just watched. He looked over his shoulder at me. "Just a sec," he said. I put the brushes down and put a chair in front of the counter facing the mirror. I turned back to him as he rose back up and turned to me. He hadn't put on the costume pants and stood there in just his cheap briefs. "OK," he smiled. "Where do you want me?"

I was again frozen in time. He stood squarely looking at me in nothing but those bunched-up, cheap underwear. Even through that ill-fitting pair, I could see the giant bulge of his junk. If I had been half-hard already, I felt a twinge in my crotch as my cock started rising to attention.

Jack's hair was messed from pulling off his t-shirt. I stuttered, "Here. Sit down." He went to grab for his costume pants but thought twice about it.

"I probably don't want to put these on, do I? Don't want to get make-up on them."

I mean, how would we get make-up on his pants? There was no reason why he couldn't put them on. "No, you're right. Leave them there. You can put them on after." He probably should put his costume shirt on before I do his make-up, too, but I couldn't bring myself to suggest it.

He sat in the metal folding chair I set for him. He flinched a little as his bare thighs landed and quipped, "Ooh, cold."

I stood before him between the counter and his knees. I set to work laying out the cakes of make-up, brushes, the hairspray. I turned back to him, and he looked up at me expectantly. His hands were on his thighs—those big, muscular thighs. I looked down at them, not a hair to be found. I traced my eyes up his entire body slowly, lingering on every inch of his male model body. I started to get very self-conscious and knew I had to cover up my staring, "OK, well, I don't think we have to worry about more than your face and neck."

"But I have a bunch of scenes where I'm shirtless," he said.

"Oh, right. Well, I guess I'll just have to blend it in down your neck and into your chest. It won't be a problem if I match your skin tone."

I set to work rubbing foundation into his skin. The fucker didn't have a single blemish, not a pimple to be found. As the sponge rubbed into the skin of his neck in my hand, I could feel the tight muscles. His neck was thick and meaty. I wanted to suck on it. I wanted to run my tongue in the base of his neck. I rubbed the sponge into it and felt my cock twinge.

I let the sponge explore down below his collar bone and onto the mounds of his pecs. I probably spent way too much time slowly sliding over them with my hands. I had this one opportunity to grope a hot frat boy's muscular chest, and I wasn't going to stop until I had to. That's when he shifted in the chair, and I knew I had reached that moment of too much.

I went on to pencils and color. Selecting what I thought best from the collection I had laid out on the counter, I leaned closer into Jack.

Putting my face into his, I looked at the lines of his forehead, the sides of his eyes, his cheeks. He just stared into my eyes. "OK, here we go," I said. And without thinking about it, I put my hand on his shoulder. I had never been so attracted to a guy in my life. Why did it have to be this totally straight, frat boy? Why did he have to be such a good guy? Why did he have to be so nice? Why was he staring into my eyes with an expectant look? I knew it was just because of the work I was doing on his make-up and not because he felt any energy between us. I was electrified. He was calm.

I looked down at my handy work after a while. It looked good. I don't want to brag, but it did. Up close he looked like a frat boy in make-up, but I knew on the stage, the exaggerated lines would wash out in the lighting, and with the distance between the audience and him, it would look good.

"OK, now your hair," I said. I pulled the spray bottle of gray coloring off the counter along with a towel. "Now hold this over your face." He took the towel from me and covered his face with it.

"Like this," he asked.

"Great. Now I'm going to spray your hair, so keep it there."

His face was covered. He couldn't see. This was my chance to get in all the gawking I wanted to. I looked him up and down. His perfect arms were held up to his face holding the towel. I took in his neck, his chest, those abs. Then looking down I took a more detailed look at that giant bulge of a package. I squinted and studied it. I could see the roundness of his balls slouched down between his legs, resting on the metal folding chair. They looked so big, so meaty. And above them I could see his cock outlined in the fabric. Even completely soft, I could make it out, folded over and pointing down over those balls. I dreamed of reaching out and grabbing it in my hands. Or kneeling down and planting my face between those huge thighs and licking the entire thing with my tongue. "Everything all right," he asked.

"Yeah, yeah. Sorry, the nozzle is sticking." I lied. Then I sprayed one blast into the air. "There, there, I got it."

I got to work on his hair. I put my hands through it and felt its silkiness. It was a deep red, almost auburn, though I only ever know women to use that color name for their hair. I probably caressed it a little too long, but hey, I was the make-up artist here. I had to think about what I was doing. I made a questioning sigh so he knew I was thinking. I didn't want him to look super old, just like middle aged. I sprayed around his temples and over his ears. I reached up and took his hair back in my hands and stroked the long strands on top of his head through my fingers.

He sighed. He fucking sighed. Then through the towel, he said, "That kinda feels nice."

I had to make a joke about this, or I was doomed. "Hey, don't get fresh with me. I'm a professional."

He pulled the towel away from his eyes and looked right at me. "Why do you think I hired you?" He kept looking at me. I smiled and pushed the towel back in his face. Did I sense a relaxing in his legs? Did he pull them apart a little bit more? I had to make more of this than it was. I took a step closer to him. I put one leg between the two of his and one leg to the side of his chair. I took one more step in and straddled his thigh.

He had to feel me there that close to him, but I kept at my work on his hair. I moved my thigh closer to his so they touched. It turned me on like crazy that he had his face buried in a towel and couldn't see me. "Are you almost done," he asked.

I sprayed a few more strands on top of his head and breathed out loudly. "There," I announced.

He took the towel away from his face. That beautiful face appeared again, looking up at me. For one quick second, he looked at my legs straddling his then back up at me. "So," he asked. "How do I look?"

"Amazing," I said too quickly. "No, seriously, it looks really good. Take a look." And with hesitation screaming through my head, I backed away from him and let him see himself in the mirror.

"Oh fuck. No way." He smiled and turned his head this way and that, looking at himself. "Shit. Look at that. He reached up to touch his hair."

"Don't touch it. It's still a little wet."

He turned to me, and with a bit of seriousness, he asked, "So is this what I'm gonna look like when I get old, do you think?"

I smiled. "Only if you keep working out," I joked. I half joked. I regretted calling attention to his body, but he smiled.

Holding up his arms and flexing his biceps, he said, "Like what you see?" He turned a little and flexed more.

I laughed and turned back to the make-up. "Get over yourself, stud. You know you're hot."

I didn't want our time all alone to end, but he reached over and pulled on his costume pants. I died inside a little, wishing he would stay almost naked a little while longer, but the moment was over. I put the make-up back in order, closed the cakes, and by the time I was done, he was in full costume and looked amazing.

"So how are things with Janine," I broke the tension that only I felt.

He looked at me confused. "Oh, there's nothing between us."

"But you took her home the night of the party, didn't you?"

He looked surprised, probably he didn't think I would have noticed or remembered.

"Oh, yeah. That was a fun night. Yeah, I walked her home. But nothing happened." He looked like that was a regret for him.

"Your choice or hers," I asked. Maybe I was prying, but I didn't care.

He hesitated. "Um, well, it just didn't work out, you know?"

"I get it." I really didn't want to talk about Janice any way, so I dropped it.

I was about to leave. I did have a lot of work to do getting ready for curtain, but Jack kept talking, "She didn't want to, you know, do it."

Oh fuck, he was talking to me about girls? And sex? "Well, you had just met, right? That was like the first night you were hanging out."

"No, I mean, at first she wanted to," Jack said. He sounded almost embarrassed. "But then, she freaked out." Oh fucking hell, I did not want to hear about any straight on straight sexual tension. I had enough of my own.

"Well, you know, girls. They change their minds. You gotta respect that."

"Oh," he stammered. "I know, I know. I didn't mean that. I mean, well..." he trailed off.

"What," I asked.

"She freaked out because she said it was too big."

I almost threw up in my mouth. I almost fell over. I lost all the breath in my lungs. "I'm sorry?"

"My dick. She said it was too big." He looked at me. I didn't know what to say. I stood there unable to move, unable to respond. All I wanted to scream out was, show me, show me.

After an interminable amount of time, I saw he was still just looking me in the eyes. I had to escape, or I was going to say something completely inappropriate. "Well, I don't know about that. I'm gay. You know what we always say. There's no such thing as too big." I thought it would be something funny to say, but he just kept looking at me. I couldn't do it. I couldn't stay. I had the immediate urge to flee, so I pulled the door of the men's dressing room open and escaped.

What was I doing, I thought to myself. That was everything I could have wanted to happen right there. And I tore out of there like a scared little boy. Did I just make it incredibly awkward for Jack?

But as I got to work on the props and set pieces for the show, there was only one thing that kept going through my mind over and over. I want to see it. I want to see it. I want to see it.

The final dress rehearsal went as well as it could have with the terrible play we were putting on. At least the actors refrained from laughing at the cheesiest lines for the first time since they'd been practicing.

As the last line was spoken, Spence called out from the audience where he had watched the whole thing without stopping them. "OK, fifteen minutes to get changed. Then back out for notes."

The cast all together descended on the two dressing rooms while I collected all the props and returned them to their original places. The set crew put the stage back to the first scene in anticipation for the next night's opening, and I had everything back where it needed to be before the cast started reappearing and taking seats in the audience. Jack was the last out, looking like he had tried to wash his hair in the bathroom sink. His red hair lay in flops all around his head, still wet, and his make-up was mostly gone, but you could still see traces of it. Looking around, I realized most of the cast looked the same.

Jay sat next to me. Spence gave the actors their notes. He was kind for the most part, knowing the dialogue they were working with was shit. In the end, he closed his notebook and asked, "OK, so how does everyone feel it went? Are you ready?"

The actors had minor comments and complaints about timing issues and ways to say their lines. Spence addressed them. I tried to look over at Jack several times, but he didn't look my way at all. Finally, Spence announced, "OK, then everyone. If there's nothing else, then same time tomorrow."

Jack raised his hand. "Um, Professor Lancaster?"

"Spence," Spence corrected him. "What is it, Jack?"

"Um," he paused then turned to me. "I just wanted to make sure Erik can help me with my make-up again." He turned his head to me. Everyone looked at me.

Spence looked over at me. "Erik? Are you good to help Jack again?"

I looked over at Jack. At last he was looking right at me. And he looked so damn fucking hot. "Yeah," I said. "Yeah, no problem."

Spence ended the meeting with a resigned tone. "Good. It looks incredible. Might be the best thing on this stage, but don't tell the chairman I said that. We should be all set then. Good luck everyone. Break legs."

The cast went out for dinner at a crappy Irish pub near campus. I went to pick Jay up in his dorm room, and Arthur met us outside, and we made our way to Peter's apartment before heading to the restaurant, so we were the last to arrive.

Jay was the first to lay into me. "So, how is it doing Jack's make-up? Shit, just the two of you alone in the dressing room for like an hour? Getting all close. Touching him. You must be dying."

I laughed, but Peter chimed in before I could say anything, "Yeah, fuck you by the way, you know meatheads are my thing. I don't know if I could it. I'd jump his bones the minute I had a chance."

I cleared my throat and couldn't get words out before Arthur did, "So did you?"

"Did I what," I asked.

"Try anything," Arthur said. All three of them were looking at me.

"What was I gonna try? He's straight."

They giggled and made sounds. "Yeah, but what did you talk about," Jay asked.

I shrugged. I didn't know what to say. Oh you know, his big, giant cock. How it's so big it scares women. "The show mostly."

Jay let out a dejected sound. "That sounds thrilling."

But that seemed to end the conversation. When we got to the restaurant, most of the cast was ensconced in a very long table, and the only spots available were all the way on one end, and Jack was on the other. Janine was on one side of him. Another girl from the show, Liz, was on his other side. Chrissy, another girl, was across from him, and all three were chewing his ear off about the show and their parts and his acting ability.

The four of us sat together at the other end and fell into our usual banter, and none of my friends even thought about Jack the entire night. I sat pretty quiet, only one thing going through my mind again and again. I wonder how big is too big.

You know straight boys. They always brag about themselves. I think every one of them thinks his cock is the best cock ever. Who's to say what Jack thought was big? He could have been making it up just to get a rise out of me, just to build himself up. Maybe he thought six inches was huge. How many cocks could he have ever seen any way?

But I'd seen the bulge, and I knew something was there, and my mind would not stop. That night I think I jerked off at least three times thinking about Jack and being alone with him in the dressing room. I pictured him in his underwear, standing up, bending me over the counter, and fucking me with his huge dick.

I pictured kneeling down in front of him and opening up his cheap underwear and blowing him while he held a towel over his face. Think about a chick, I would say to him before going down on his big, fat cock.

The next day Jay, Arthur, Peter, and I skipped all our classes, like we did on opening night for every show. We went shopping for new outfits to wear to the opening night cast party, which was going to be at Peter's place. In the afternoon, Jay went to the liquor store and bought a half-keg. The rest of us went to the store and bought chips and snacks. Peter positioned his speakers around the room and thought about music options, and before I knew it, I saw it was 4:30.

"Oh shit, guys. I gotta get to the theater."

"Oh, yeah, you gotta be early to do your boyfriend," Jay joked.

"Holy fuck, I wish," I said.

Before I could get out the door, Arthur said, "I bet he has a big one."

There I was again. In the dressing room alone with Jack. There were no brushes to run off and find, so I just stood there as he undressed and watched. It might have made him slightly awkward, but I didn't care. After the last full day of my mind thinking about nothing else, I just stood there and waited while he pulled off all his clothes in front of me. Surprisingly, he was again willing to get all the way down to his underwear in front of me again, and even more surprising, he had much better underwear on. But when he bent over, and I got a look at them, my mind went wild. He was wearing a skimpy pair of low-rise, light blue briefs. But they were one of those sporty brands deemed acceptable by straight dudes everywhere. I looked at his ass when he bent over. Half of it was fully visible. The flesh of it a bright pale. Those two globes shone at me in all their muscular glory, and then he turned around, and there it was. That huge bulging package. Only this time it was even more obvious, all jammed together in a smaller pouch.

He sat down. I couldn't not say anything. "No granny panties tonight?"

His eyes went wide. "What? Oh, you mean, yeah. Um, my mom bought those other ones. They suck, don't they?"

I laughed. "Yeah, dude. Maybe that's why chicks won't fuck you."

He fake-punched me in the stomach as I pulled in close in front of him. "Hey, I get mine."

As I started to work on his dreamy neck, I was leaning in close. I realized he was staring into my eyes. "So what about you," he asked.

"Huh? What about me?"

"Do you get any?"

I hesitated. "Well, um, I guess." But then I added. "It's a little tough. There's not a lot of gay guys here."

He shrugged. "Yeah, I guess not. But what about Jay? Aren't you two an item? I see the way he looks at you."

"What? No. He's my best friend. We fooled around once when we first met, but no, it's not like that."

"Oh, cool."

I didn't know what he meant by that, but I continued to work on his make-up. While I was about to start on the lines around his eyes, I found him looking right at me again. "I'm sorry about yesterday," he said.

"What do you mean?"

"I mean, about Janine. And telling you about what she said. That was rude, I think."

"It's no big deal," I said.

"OK, it's just, I didn't want you to think I was bragging is all."

I drew the pencil across the side of his eye and applied age lines. "We all think our cock is the biggest." What the fuck did I just say?

I could hear him breathe in. "Well, I just didn't want it to be weird between us."

I hemmed and hawed, "It's cool. And here I thought you were just a big, dumb frat guy."

He laughed, which made me smudge the line I was working on. "Oh. I am," he said.

I fixed my mistake and did a pretty damn good job on the rest of his make-up, if I do say so myself. Then it was time for his hair. While he had the towel over his face, I looked back down at that package of his. I hadn't even grabbed the spray can yet. I just stood there, looking at it. Fuck, damn, hell. This boy did not just have a huge cock. There were those balls in there, too. And it was all right there. Cock trailing to the right this time instead of folded down. Believe me, I'm a connoisseur of looking at packages.

I looked at that treasure trail of red hair that pointed right at it. I looked all over his body. I realized it had been an awkward amount of time, but I was loving having him sit there in front of me almost completely naked, holding that towel over his face. Finally I turned to pick up the hairspray when I heard him shift in his chair and clear his throat.

"Nine."

What did he say? I was pretty sure of what he had said, but I needed to hear it again.

"What?"

His face still buried in the towel, he repeated, "It's nine."

I didn't say anything just looked back down at it. Was it looking at me?

He took the towel off his face and caught me staring at his bulge, mouth opened. "It's nine inches. So is that big?"

I couldn't pull my eyes away, and he'd already caught me staring, but hey, he had brought it up, so I wasn't going to pretend I wasn't looking. "Yeah. That's big.'

He put the towel back over his face. "Told you so."

I finished up his hair. I again came in close. This time I straddled his leg after he'd already tossed the towel away, so he saw me do it. I ruffled my fingers through his hair. The spray was still a little wet, but I didn't care. I looked at his make-up. It looked good.

"There you're done." I stepped back. He stood up and looked at my work in the mirror over my shoulder. I turned around for some reason to look at his reflection, too, instead of at him directly.

"So," he said. "I couldn't have done this without you. How am I gonna repay you?"

I blurted it out without even thinking. My mind didn't have time to stop my mouth. My mouth was listening to another part of my body. I looked at his eyes in the mirror and said, "You can show it to me."

"What?" He put a little sheepish tone on his voice, but he smiled wide. I turned back around to face him square on, inches in front of him. His hands trailed down his torso. I saw his fingers reach that amazing treasure trail. Two slid into the waistband of his briefs.

I didn't say anything. I wasn't letting him off the hook. We just looked at each other, and as his other hand started to reach in for that bulge, the door burst open, and two of the male cast members crashed into the room. "Hey," one of them said.

"Hey," I replied. You fucking fucks, could your timing be any worse?

But when my eyes came away from the newcomers and back to Jack, he was already turned around putting his costume on. Fuck.

Opening night was actually not as bad as I imagined it was going to be. None of Jack's frat friends ended up coming to the show, but the audience that was there, mostly other arts students trying to kiss up to our chairman, some faculty that you know felt obligated to go, and old people from the local town, seemed to enjoy it. There was a solid applause for the show and the leads. So everyone was in a great mood.

After greeting theatergoers after the show, the actors washed up in the dressing rooms while I roamed all over the house collecting props and things. I couldn't find the boxing gloves, so I was going all over backstage and onstage looking for them. They were nowhere to be found. I went into the men's dressing room while they were all changing. I called over, "Jack, where are your boxing gloves?"

He was changing but looked over at me and shrugged, "I don't know. Didn't I leave them on stage?"

"No. I can't find them anywhere," I said. He shrugged.

Cast members one by one as they finished changing left the theater. They called out, "See you at the cast party." I waved or nodded and answered in agreement, but I was really stressing over where the damn gloves could be.

It got quieter and quieter. Spence left and asked me if I was good.

"I can't find the boxing gloves," I lamented.

Spence, usually the nicest professor you could imagine, just stared at me before leaving and said, "Well you better find them. We need them."

I went backstage. This wasn't going to be good. If the gloves were lost, we had five more shows to get through. Fuck. I went to the women's dressing room and knocked. "I'm coming in," I called out.

As I opened the door, I said, "Has anybody seen the gloves..," but as I opened the door, I realized everyone was already gone.

I went to the men's dressing room and walked in without announcing myself. Jay was putting his jacket on but was the only one there. "Hey, have you seen those fucking boxing gloves?"

He just shrugged at me. "No. They're not in here. What are you going to do?"

I was sweating. "I don't know. Fuck, am I gonna have to go out tomorrow and buy a new pair?"

Jay picked up his bag and smiled at me. "Don't stress out, dude. We have a party to go to. Worry about it tomorrow."

"Yeah, you're right. I'll see you in a few," I said, and Jay left.

I went back out into the theater and looked around one last time. Nothing. It was going to have to be dealt with tomorrow. I was left all alone, and I now just really needed a fucking beer. I went back to the men's dressing room to grab my coat, and as soon as I threw the door, there in the middle of the room stood Jack. Hot, muscular Jack. In nothing but his underwear.

I stared at him. He was grinning at me like crazy. "We were interrupted," he said.

I let the door close.

"What are you doing?"

He stepped closer to me. took me by the arm and spun me over to the chair. The chair he always sat in for me to do his make-up. He pushed me down into it and stood over me, our usual positions reversed.

I looked from his eyes to his neck, that beautiful neck, now freshly cleaned of make-up, down to that chest, those abs, oh god, those abs.

Then my eyes lingered down that red treasure trail and to that bulge. That amazing bulge was there again, but now it was clearly bigger.

Now that cock was trailing along to the side under the waistband. He was clearly hard, at least harder than he'd been before. I looked back up to his eyes. He was looking down at me. "We had a deal."

I realized I wasn't breathing. We just stood there, two college guys, one gay, one straight frat boy, alone. "What," I said.

He said, "You said I should show it to you."

"Well," I had to go for it. "That was before."

"What do you mean?"

I cleared my throat, and with every cell inside my brain screaming at me to take advantage of the situation, I reached up and put my hand on that huge bulge inches from my face. "I deserve more than just a look."

A huge grin appeared across Jack's face. Fuck, he was hot. Now with that smile and that look of devilish intent on his face, he said, "What did you have in mind?"

"You have to let me suck it."

Silence. Jack looked at me. I looked at him. My hand was resting on his big cock. Through the fabric of his underwear, I could feel the girth of it, the length. Damn, this was a grade A piece of meat. He didn't say anything. I went for it. I reached up and pulled on the elastic waistband.

I pulled slowly. I saw his cock bunch down, getting compressed. I put two fingers inside the top of his briefs and pulled, and that cock sprung out at me. Oh fuck it was beautiful. He was uncut. I saw a huge head covered in his foreskin. His balls were shaved clean of what would have been a red bush. What straight boy shaves his balls? It bobbed out and stuck straight out in front of my face.

I didn't hesitate another single second. I opened my mouth wide and slid down on it. I pushed my face down on that huge pink cock and stretched my lips around it. "Fuck," Jack sighed out.

I wrapped my hand around the base of it. Jack put his hands down onto his hips and pushed his briefs down around his thighs. I squeezed my lips tight on the top of his cock and rang my tongue around the skin.

I pulled it back out and pulled down with my hand at the base, and his head appeared out of the skin. I pulled some more so it was uncovered completely. Fuck it was the most beautiful thing I'd ever seen. I opened wide and slid my mouth down on it. It was huge, everything I'd ever wanted, and it was disappearing into my mouth. I tried to relax my throat and kept pushing until it slid down further.

"Fuck," Jack said again. I started to slide up and down on his unbelievable cock. I put my other hand around and grabbed his big round ass and pulled it toward me while I pushed my face down on him.

I pumped up and down on him but couldn't get the whole cock down my throat. It was just way too long. I was a total size queen, and I thought if I can't, no one can. After a while, I felt a huge amount of precum soaking my own cock in my shorts. I didn't know what this straight frat boy would think of me taking mine out, so I didn't.

He put his hands on the back of my head and started thrusting. He started pumping his cock in and out of my mouth. Every now and then, he let out another simple, "Fuck."

He was tossing his head back. I reached up and put my hands all over him. I grabbed his chest, his lats, his abs. I reached around and grabbed the big meaty orbs of his butt in both my hands. I was going to enjoy this body. I traced a finger down the crack of his ass. That was a real test. Was he going to react against me touching his butt? The moan he let out told me no.

I was in heaven. He appeared to be loving it. I started caressing his balls while he face-fucked me. That seemed to be putting him over the edge. It felt like forever. I never wanted it to end. But after a while, his breathing changed. He took his hands off the back of my head. I didn't stop sucking him. I looked up at him. He looked down at me. "Oh baby," he sighed. He looked at me with a pleading look.

He gave me a warning. He sighed out. "I'm gonna..," he said. I didn't stop sucking him. "I'm gonna," he said again. I grabbed his ass again and pushed myself down on his huge cock as deep as I could so he understood. I didn't want to stop.

"Fuck," he whispered. And then he let loose. He was buried in my throat, and I could feel the pulsing blast. For one moment, I stayed planted hard, but I wanted to taste him, so I pulled out all but the head, and his second and third and fourth blast flooded my mouth with salty passion.

His body stopped convulsing. I looked up at him and saw him look right into my eyes. He looked like every nerve in his body was alive. I pushed some of his cum out over my lower lip and let it dribble down my chin. I thought that would look hot. I licked his cock then his balls. I let more cum pour out of my mouth so he could see it.

Then he did something I absolutely did not expect. He bent over and planted his mouth on mine. He gave me a passionate kiss. His lips opened to mine. His tongue darted into my cum-soaked mouth, and he shared the taste of himself from my lips. His arms were around my shoulders, and he kept kissing me for a while. His hand came to the back of my neck. I reached up and put mine around his. He pulled me up and wrapped his arms around me, and I felt his hard body pressed against mine.

He reached around and cupped my ass in his hand. Finally he stopped kissing me, and with one hand, he caressed my face.

"Let's get you cleaned up," he whispered. "We have a party to get to."

I smiled at him. I was doe-eyed. I was in the dream-like fog of the moments after. But he pulled away and turned to retrieve his clothes. I went into the dressing room bathroom and washed my face and gargled a little water. I finished washing and went back out to the dressing room.

Jack picked up his knapsack from the closet. He put it on the counter. "Oh," he said and pulled the boxing gloves out of his bag. "Were you looking for these?'

He was smiling at me with a giant toothy grin. I let out a laugh. He tossed them to me. "Well, I had to figure out some way to get you alone," he said.

"I was going crazy looking for these," I complained at him, though I was not at all upset.

"Well, sorry about that," he said and got that devilish look on his face again. "How can I make it up to you?"

Freshman Orientation

by Michael Roberts

I hated the spring.

I was beginning my college career at the start of the 1970s and looking forward to a different environment than the one I was used to. Well, the environment was different, but I wasn't. I was still confused about who I might be and what I felt and what I wanted, and I was damned horny. I'd made it through the winter without scattering into a billion or so pieces like a burst balloon, but now spring had sprung and the sap was rising, and I was about to become sprung, and my sap was rising, and I hated the spring.

Sure, the guys stopped swaddling themselves in heavy coats and scarves, but it was worse to see them in long shorts riding low on their hips and showing the beginning of the triangle that led to their crotches, or pulled down past their underwear, tighty whiteys, or patterned boxers, sometimes shoved even farther, revealing the tips of butt cracks, tee shirts plastered against firm pectorals or short sleeved shirts bouncing unbuttoned in the breeze to display hirsute or un-hirsute chests, or sometimes no shirt at all, open to the air and hypnotized eyesight, or tennis shorts just half an inch away from total revelation, anchored by bountiful bulges straining against barely restrictive fabric.

I hated it.

I was led around by my rampant dick, aimed like a Geiger counter, here to perky nipples, there to enticing protuberances, bouncing off trees I hadn't seen, tripping on rocks I didn't expect, colliding occasionally with a co-ed who batted me away like an irritating insect or an annoyed male who threatened to connect his fist with my nose.

Did I mention I hated it?

I would have jerked off every night for some sort of relief, but my roommate and I slept together—well, not together together but on separate single beds with a stand and a lamp between us. And when I thought that he was asleep, I prepared to express my sexual frustration wetly, but then he would snort or change position or not snore, and in the quiet, I became sure that he was awake and could not mistake what I was doing, and I stilled my hand between my legs and tried to ignore my blue balls and occasionally managed to drift into uneasy slumber.

The next day, I would be sure he regarded me with knowing, and maybe pitying, eyes or perhaps a sneer, and I'd smile weakly and go off after a night of not getting off to pinging between longing and frustrating encounters with the unapproachable and the unattainable, and I hated it, I hated it, I hated it.

I had anesthetized myself against Roy's attractions, which he certainly did possess. He was handsome and well groomed, and he had an engaging smile, but I resisted getting engaged, because he also had a girlfriend. There were nights he was absent from the apartment and returned home late, if at all. Some of those nights, I lay feigning sleep, facing his side of the room, wondering what pulsed beneath his pajama bottoms, which he wore with or without tops, depending on the weather, and the sight of him pulling back covers and settling for bed, the muscles of his back rippling, which I envisioned even if they were covered, and the momentary presentation of his backside in my direction, even if encased in fabric, excited my erogenous feelings, and it became all the more difficult not to propel myself into erotic overflowing.

Oh, I hated it.

That year was the last one that freshmen were not required to live on campus. Neither Roy nor I wanted to be in a dorm, so though we didn't know each other well, we decided to rent together. More than once I regretted my decision, considering that Roy was, as they say, as

I definitely realized, so near and yet so very far. He was a nice guy, and that was part of the problem.

Our apartment was about a mile from the university. It was up a flight of stairs, above another apartment, and across from us was a third apartment. Three football players lived there—Mike, Jim, and Carl.

As the semester progressed, Roy and I became friendly with the three athletes, who were juniors. Mike was a quarterback, Jim was in the backfield, and Carl was a lineman. They didn't have much in common with Roy and me, and our conversations were limited to pleasantries when we encountered each other leaving or arriving at the apartment building.

They were pleasing to the eyes, at least to my admittedly roving eyes. Mike had the arrogant good looks of someone whom a team would happily follow to victory or defeat. Jim was the sort of handsome frat guy to whom the co-eds and assorted others flocked. And Carl had a sort of smashed magnetism.

One afternoon, I walked home from class. Roy had a car, and often I could catch a ride with him. Today was not one of those times, so instead of studying in the student union, as I frequently did, I set out on foot. What began as a pleasantly warm stroll turned quickly into a slow hot trudge as the temperature rose and the sun became malicious. This was more like the steamy middle of summer. I hated spring.

The three teammates were at the top of the stairs. Two of them were holding six packs of beer. We said hello and exchanged comments about the weather, and then Mike asked, "Want a beer?"

"Sure," I said, and I waited for them to open their door, and it became obvious they were waiting for me to open my door, which I did, and we trundled into my place. I went to the living room window to turn on the air conditioner, and when I looked back, they were sitting on the rather ratty sofa Roy and I had acquired from an alley, and they watching me. I sort of expected one of them to put his hands over his mouth and one of them to put his hands over his eyes and one of them to put his hands over his ears, but they didn't, they just stared at me. I reached out a hand, and after a moment while they seemed to decide what I wanted, Jim gave me a can, and I popped its tab and sat in the easy chair that had also been a rescue and took a sip.

We four regarded one another, and Mike opened a beer and drank, and Jim opened a beer and drank, and Carl opened a beer and drank, like an assembly line, and I drank, and we sat in silence, and just as I was ready to ask them how football practice was going, Mike said, "We're thinking about getting a whore."

Pause.

Then he laughed and said, "I didn't mean one of those girls who hang around practice and hope to score a field goal."

The three of them laughed far more, I thought, than Mike's comment warranted.

"No," Mike said after the falsely raucous merriment died down. "I mean someone who does it for a living."

Raised eyebrows and leers.

"You interested?"

"Uh...," I cleverly riposted.

The three looked at me.

I looked at them.

"Or maybe we don't need to pay someone," said Mike. "Maybe we've got somebody here who—well—who—you know."

He rubbed his crotch.

For a moment, I didn't know. And then I did know—I thought.

"Why do I—why do you," I managed to ask through my dry mouth.

Mike shrugged.

"We're kinda used to chicks—and dudes—admiring us. And we think that you—admire us."

"Yeah," added Jim. "We've noticed you watching us."

"Hmm," I commented, continuing my witty repartee.

"Are we wrong?" asked Carl.

"Nnnnnno," I gurgled.

"Are you interested?"

"Yyyyyes," I gurgled.

As if choreographed, the three guys bent over and slipped out of their shoes, leaving on their socks as if we were in an old-fashioned porno film. Then they stood and shimmied out of their pants and underwear and draped the clothing over the back of the sofa. Ready for action—my action—they plopped down in unison, three cocks at attention.

Mike's and Jim's cocks were certainly attractive, an appetizing size and shape. Carl's was shorter—not short, just shorter—and broader—and looked as if it could drive back whatever lineman was facing him, perhaps the entire line. Mike spread his legs and looked at me expectantly.

I knelt before him and took him in my mouth.

I had wondered how dick would taste. I found it quite pleasing to the palate. It was a bit odd, sucking some guy while two other guys watched and stimulated themselves, but I adapted, especially after Mike moaned a few times. Evidently my technique was satisfactory. Mike's prick was certainly satisfactory.

I went over the length and breadth of Mike's fleshy extension, applying some moves I'd observed in videos and some others that just seemed right—top, bottom, tip, vacuuming, tongue, lips, and so forth. The so-forth made Mike even more rigid. Twice I made it all the way down his dick, which was nice for both of us if Mike's exclamations were any evidence.

I was getting quite lost in the pleasure of taste and feel when Mike grabbed my head, pulled it to his pubis, and exploded in my mouth.

His detonation was thick, salty, and tangy. It was, of course, the first time I had sampled cum. It was definitely a dietary delight, and after I'd rolled it around a bit, I swallowed. Ingest, then digest. Later, I learned each man's discharge tastes different—but that's another story.

A trickle of Mike's foam dribbled from one side of my mouth, and Mike traced it with a finger, then dangled it in front of me. I licked the drops of his enthusiastic response to my oral efforts, and he grinned and shuffled me off to Jim.

My mouth was coated with Mike's generous offering, so I couldn't at once discern Jim's unique flavor. I did immediately note that Jim's johnson had a bend just before the tip, leaning to his right, my left, so that each traversal downward was like a short detour before I got back on the main thoroughfare upward.

And as I steered along Jim's dick, I replaced Mike's essence with more and more of Jim's particular piquancy, and so I was finding that men's pricks were diverse—at least in my limited experience.

It was surely part of my limited experience to feel my own cock straining against my underwear and pants. I mean, I had rather often experienced a stiffening cock calling attention to itself but only at my own instigation, burgeoning because of my burgeoning imagination, or inadvertently if I were stimulated by the presence, the sight, the smell of some attractive male or somewhat attractive male or more than occasionally any male at all, but this was the first time my dick had developed an elevation because of my involvement with another man. I said hello to this prickly phenomenon by massaging the front of my lower self as I took a side trip to Jim's balls, which, oddly enough, were shaved—well, surely I was not the only person, of whatever persuasion, who had slurped these sexual sacs, and maybe that was how other suckers preferred them. Or maybe that was the way he preferred them. My acquaintance with a backfield in motion was limited, especially a backfield with a dick in my mouth. Anyway, these gonads were intriguing, and I explored them for a while—even got both of them in my mouth together—and then returned to the main highway.

I glanced up at Jim's face, and he had laid his head on the back of the sofa and closed his eyes. He started to hum, and his body rose and straightened, and I thought that I was going to get my second helping of gism, but he pushed me away from him and transferred me to Carl.

I was prepared to continue my comparison shopping and discover how Carl's flavor differed from Jim's and Mike's, but Carl didn't allow me that sampling. From the moment his dick delved into my dentistry, Carl was on the attack—literally.

He fucked my face. He dove into my mouth and battered away forcefully. I had noted that his cock was somewhat shorter than the other two, but it was wider, and it insisted that my mouth assume a different configuration, stretching open as far as it could go and further, in all directions, up and down and side to side, as he commanded, "Watch those teeth!" Well, he was a lineman, so I should have expected him to attack and block and tackle and dispose of any defense I might have, and I didn't have much, I just hoped that the configuration of my mouth would not be permanently altered, perhaps destroyed, by its force and speed. I did get some liquid stimulation as jets of his juice spurted into my mouth, but that delight was transitory as the next swing of his hammer swiped it away. And his teammates cheered him on, yelling "Go, Carl!" and "Get him, Carl!" And he got me and got me and got me.

Abruptly he stopped and withdrew, and he got up and pulled me to my feet and grinned as widely as his cock and undid my belt buckle and shoved my pants to the floor and nearly ripped me out of my underwear and slid a hand from the bottom of my shirt to the top, dispensing of the buttons and then dispensing of the shirt, and pulled me toward the bedroom, and I stumbled along with him, attempting not to fall over my shoes and the trousers around my ankles. Carl catapulted me face first onto the bed, and Jim, who was now totally nude, stretched out on top of me and spread my cheeks, my butt cheeks this time, and entered me.

I knew it was Jim, because he put his hands on the pillow beside my head, and I recognized his bracelet, and the intrusion into my interior was—well, not quite gentle, under the circumstances, but relatively gentle, as if Jim was allowing me to accustom myself as he explored my previously unexplored regions. I first had to adjust to the pain of his bent cock descending into me and then to the feeling of fullness and then to his movement within me.

Vaguely, I was aware that someone was removing my shoes and pulling my pants off my legs, and since I hadn't worn an undershirt and since Carl had engineered my striptease, I became, thus, as utterly naked as Jim sliding back and forth inside me, and his movement and my lying totally unclothed beneath him, exposed to him and exposed, in more ways than one, to the two spectators who were expecting their time in my saddle, made my cock stretch and harden under me and emit an expression of my excitement onto my bedspread.

Jim began to breathe more loudly, and the pace of his fucking sped up, and the warmth of his dick diving into me increased, and he stopped all the way in me and shouted in my ear and shot inside me.

He lay atop me, and I felt his chest and stomach rising and falling against my back, and Mike called out, "All right, Jim, give somebody else a turn."

Jim chuckled and rolled off me, and Mike rolled on.

Mike banged me like a quarterback, roaring back and projecting his passes with unerring accuracy. I was hardly (so to speak) his wide receiver, but I was definitely widening to receive his well-thrown attacks. His cock scored and scored in my end zone, completing every touchback, touchdown, and field goal, and some extra yardage besides. He was racking up the points and racking and rocking me, score, score, score.

I had moaned underneath Jim and was barking beneath Mike, and his cheering section pushed him on, yelling "Go, Mike, go!" And he went and went on and then went further, and my dick drove moistly into the bed, and in exaltation he made his final attack and shouted in conquest and exploded within me. Then he collapsed on my back and whispered in my ear, "I've got some other teammates who would like to meet you."

And he and some of his fellow players dropped in on me one day and—but that's another story.

Mike dismounted, and Carl climbed aboard. I had dreaded and anticipated this third volley of dickhood, and I tried to steel myself, realizing that no amount of preparation could protect me from the good and the bad and the unknown to follow.

Carl grabbed my hips and pulled me into a doggie position, and then he did me. He was brutal, and I craved the brutality. He showed no mercy, and I wanted no mercy. Carl attacked and jabbed and stoked hotly into me. Sometimes he withdrew entirely and then plunged his length and width with what seemed lighting quickness back inside me in a single stab, letting my assaulted ass relax and then crashing into it, insisting that I accept the thick crown and the rotund root or not accept them because in any case they were there and damn his torpedo full speed ahead.

His fellow players were clapping rhythmically like the crowd clapping in the final few moments of the game, wanting one more score.

I wished his assault would stop, and I wished it would go on, and it went on and on until I was sure that I was splitting down the middle, and just when I knew that I couldn't take this warfare an additional minute, an additional second, Carl roared and made that final score and geysered into me, and I felt it all the way to my teeth, and he collapsed onto me.

Panting, he stayed inside me for a while, perhaps appreciating his conquest. Then he exclaimed, "Wow!" And he exited my battered back door with an audible plop and stood up to an appreciative response from his fans.

I'm sure that neither he nor his teammates knew or might have cared that goaded into my own sexual fervor by the two men who preceded him and then by Carl's barrage upon my physical self and my mental and psychological self, below Carl I had reached another release. My bucking and shaking and panting and spewing sperm onto my bed would have seemed part of Carl's frenzied fucking and his noisy and copious coming in my weary ass.

I didn't have the strength to lift the face that was buried in my bed pillow, so I just lay listening to the three football players put themselves together and leave the apartment, shouting "Thanks, dude," which I thought was nice of them.

I had been initiated into the joys and pains of sex, sucked three men and then been fucked by them, been driven to my own sensual explosion, and in the process featured in the equivalent of a live sex show. No doubt I would see my own football squad again, maybe multiple times with multiple sex games, and Mike was going to introduce me to more of his buddies, which seemed promising, and who knew what else was before me?

It was going to be a hell of a semester! And a spring, need it be stated, that I no longer hated.

I'll Do Anything

by Matthew Cooper

Dumb jock is a stereotype, I know, but in the case of Keith Taylor, it was one hundred percent spot on. He epitomized the roll to a tee. I don't want to sound mean, but this kid was as dumb as a box of rocks. But he had also been the star quarterback of the high school football team and hot as fuck.

Keith Taylor had been a neighbor of mine growing up in the shitty, dying, coal-mining town in Northeast Pennsylvania where we both grew up, and back in high school, he bullied me relentlessly. Funny thing was, he only did it when we were alone. Most bullies make fun of you or harass you in front of the other kids. They get some type of validation from it, I guess. Keith was different. For him, bullying me and only me was personal, and because of Keith Taylor, I dreaded almost every day of high school.

It didn't help that he lived right around the corner from me. He made it a point to sit next to me in class whenever there was a test, and he would copy my answers. If I tried to hide my paper from him, I knew that day after school, he'd find me in the neighborhood or even in my own backyard, and I'd be the victim of wedgies, noogies, headlocks, and a relentless barrage of names—nerd, brown-noser, faggot, pussy.

Keith Taylor was my personal nightmare, and no one in school knew it. The thing is, though, he'd relentlessly tease me, pin me down on the ground and sit on me, make fun of me, throw my books around, but he would always get to the point where he would just stop. He'd let me up, or he'd pick up my books and give them back to me. He'd mess up my hair, give me a light punch on the arm, and tell me he was just joking around.

He never really hurt me, and I tolerated all this unwanted attention for one very good reason. Keith Taylor was also hot as fuck. He was one of those dumb kids who started working out in the garage with his dad's weights when he was just 14 or 15. So by the time we were in high school, he was all muscle. He had eyes that were so dark, they looked black instead of brown. He kept his hair super short, just fuzz really, that looked really military. He had cheekbones and a jawline that could cut glass. His neck was thick, and his shoulders, arms, and chest were huge.

I secretly loved when he would grab me in those arms and pin me down and look me in the eyes and make fun of me. I probably had a hard-on every time he put me in a headlock and wouldn't let me go. Thing is, though, I never really wanted him to let go.

None of those feelings made sense to me back in high school. I didn't put it together in my head that I was gay and in love with my bully until I went off to college. I went to a faraway school out of state. Maybe it was to get away from the smalltown bullshit. But maybe it was to get away from my narrow-minded family and neighbors. Or maybe it was to get away from Keith Taylor.

At college I came into my own. I had left home and enrolled in a great school. Being smart was no longer something to be made fun of. I made friends. We grew more mature together. And most importantly, I came out. To other people but also to myself.

So imagine the turmoil of mixed emotions that coursed through me that day on campus at the start of my sophomore year when walking across the campus, I saw ahead of me none other than Keith Taylor. What the fuck was he doing here? I was walking one way. He was on the sidewalk ahead of me, coming right at me. As the distance shrunk, my heart leapt. Or maybe it sunk. I didn't know which one.

He looked at me and realized that I had been looking at him. His eyes went wide, and he called out, "Dude! What the fuck!" He practically barreled into me and enveloped me in a meathead full body hug. He was even bigger than I remembered. I was swept into his muscular arms, pulled tight to his chest, and I didn't know what to feel. His knuckle was on the top of my head, bearing down and rubbing into my scalp as he laughed, "What the fuck. Billy Peters. You fucking brainiac. You go here? No way."

"Hi Keith," was all I could say.

"Dude, I transferred here. You're looking at the newest member of the football team."

No. Please no. It couldn't be true. I made my escape. He and our shitty little hometown, it was all in the past. But here he stood in front of me on the campus that I'd made my own. A place I didn't share with anyone, the place where I'd blossomed into the start of adulthood. There I stood feeling like I was back in high school again. Keith Taylor. My bully. My torment. My secret obsession?

He told me to give him my phone number, and he tapped it into his cellphone. As always, it was impossible for me to say no. He asked me where I was living. I told him I was in the West residence hall. He asked me what room. I was helpless looking into those dark black eyes. I told him.

As he walked off, I had hopes that I wouldn't see much of him. It was a big campus. He was definitely not going to be taking the kinds of classes I was taking. He probably majored in Physical Education or General Business or some other course work that would have nothing in common with my studies in computer science.

He would be busy with football practices and games. He'd be on the road playing at other universities. He'd be hanging out with his teammates, cheerleaders, whatever dumb jocks do. I would be in the computer lab working. And for the most part, that was exactly how it was. I didn't Keith Taylor again for several weeks.

Then one day I was in the library studying in a quiet corner when I heard the voices of two guys close by. They sounded like your typical jock meatheads. Lots of 'dude' and 'bro' and 'fuck this.' I stood up from my study desk and collected my stack of books to head back to my dorm room, and as I turned a corner, I saw them at another study desk. Keith Taylor and another big muscle dude who I assumed must also be a football player. Well, actually it was kind of obvious, because they both had their letterman jackets on.

I instinctively thought about turning around, but my brain somehow didn't get that message out to my feet. They kept going toward the two football players. I had only a few seconds before Keith saw me, and instead of run the other way, after my eyes fell on the other dude, there was no turning around again. He was beautiful. He had a mop of blond hair, and his body was obviously incredibly muscular but lean, much skinnier than meathead Keith who sat in a chair at the desk facing this blond god.

I kept walking closer and closer to them. The blond dude looked over at me. For one instant, I thought he must know I'm soaking in the sight of him. I'm about to get called a faggot or worse. That's when Keith turned his head to see what Blondie was looking at. He got one look at me and called out, "Billy!"

The blond looked right at me. Keith looked right at me. I got sheepish and embarrassed, like I didn't belong. "Hi Keith."

"You know this kid," the blond god asked Keith.

He stood up and put his muscular arm around my shoulder. He pulled my head into his side and again like in high school, he was rubbing his knuckle into the top of my head. "Blake, this here's Billy. We went to high school together."

Blake. Blond boy Blake. He looked at me. I melted inside. "Hey," was all he said to me.

Keith let me go with a shove that almost made me drop my books. The two of them stared at me. I could tell Blake had no interest in knowing me. Keith sat back down. I didn't know what to say, and so of course, as awkwardly as I could, I blurted out, "I was just leaving."

Keith protested almost immediately. "No, buddy. This is perfect. I need you. You gotta help me." I didn't know where this was going, but with Keith it was never gonna be good. This guy who spent high school stealing my answers on tests—this was not going to be good at all.

I looked at him then to Blake who stared back at me like I was some kind of joke. Standing with these two muscular football hunks, I must have looked funny. At just 5 foot 5, I'm a little short. These guys were both over 6 feet tall. They were hulking muscular studs. I was skinny, short, small. I loved my tight little stomach when I looked in the mirror, but I could never put on any muscle, and I never got into lifting weights.

Keith stood up, and putting both his hands onto my shoulders, he just about picked me up and dropped me into the chair he'd vacated. I didn't know what to think, but I was now sitting, and two giant studly athletes loomed over me. I looked at Keith. He still had his military buzzcut, which made him look even more powerful and manly. I looked at Blake. His blond hair fell around his face. He also had piercing eyes and the same thick kind of neck that I guessed all football players had. His letterman jacket looked like it was probably a size too small, because it could not cover his huge chest. I could even see the thickness of his upper arms through it.

Standing over me, Keith smiled down at me. Blake seemed to be backing him up or watching to see what happens. "Buddy," Keith said, "I need your help."

"Me?" I was confused and held my books tightly to my chest.

"Billy. Dude, I can't fail any classes, or I can't play, and the team is counting on me." He looked over at Blake who nodded. "You gotta help me." I looked into Keith Taylor's eyes and for the first time ever saw concern, need, and, if you can believe it, modesty.

Blake spread his legs a little farther apart and leaned into our conversation. "You gotta help him."

I stuttered, "What can I do? Like tutor you or something?"

Keith squatted down next to me, bending his knees. He put a hand on the back of my chair. He was so much bigger than me that even squatted down and balancing on the balls of his feet, he came just about eye to eye with me. "Yeah, I mean, you could tutor me. Or I was thinking you could do this assignment for me. It's due on Friday. We have a big game on Saturday, and I can't fail."

It all came rushing back at me. This big stupid dude who made me let him copy my test answers through high school. Suddenly he was back in my life but in college now. And he wanted me to do his work for him. Why is it always the jock taking advantage of the nerd?

If I didn't stand up for myself now, this was never going to end. And if he wasn't going anywhere, and I wasn't going anywhere, we'd be on this campus for another two and a half years together.

"No fucking way, Keith. This isn't high school anymore. You can't just copy off my paper anymore." I tried to stand up, but Keith's hand went from the chair to my shoulder. Blake didn't move and seemed to loom even larger over me.

I looked Keith in the face. I knew I had a big scowl on mine. "Fuck you, Keith. Do your own work. This is ridiculous. Grow up."

He didn't let go of my shoulder. Blake boxed me in more. Blake standing over me. Keith squatted in front of me. There was no one around in this quiet back study area of the library. I didn't budge. They weren't moving. Until finally it seemed like something broke in Keith's resolve. Those dark black eyes suddenly turned soft. His brows curled, and he looked more like a puppy. I don't know how I kept my composure. The next time he spoke, suddenly his voice was subdued.

Modesty and sincerity gushed forth from Keith Taylor. He rolled forward until he was on his knees. The hand on my shoulder dropped and came to rest on my thigh. His other hand came down on my other thigh. He squeezed them both. "Please, Billy. You gotta help me. I need you. You're smart. I'm not smart. I'm fucking stupid. I can't fail."

He looked so sad and defeated, and then he added the words that made my heart skip a beat, words that I will remember for the rest of my life. "I'll do anything."

Wow. Keith Taylor was begging me. He was flattering me. He was talking to me like I mattered. "Keith, I'm not just gonna do your project for you. If you want me to help you, I will help you, but you're gonna do the work."

Suddenly Blake bent down closer to me. He also looked more crestfallen. "Dude, we need our quarterback. The paper's due on Friday. There's no time. He said he'll do anything for you."

I was so taken aback, I didn't know what to say. I tried to give a little fake laugh through my surprise. I jokingly said, "Anything?"

Blake looked around one way then the other. "He'll have sex with you."

I let out all the air in my lungs. I gave another really pathetic sounding laugh. "What? Get the fuck out of here."

Keith Taylor squeezed my thighs again. But this time it didn't feel the same. It was like there was some amount of care or connection in the touch now. He looked me right in the eyes. "I would. I'll have sex with you."

I sat speechless. Now what do I do? How could I act like that is exactly what I want, exactly what I've wanted for over five years now, that all the way back to high school, every time he pinned me down and put me in a headlock, I fantasized about being naked with him, having sex with him. That this very moment was more than I ever could have dreamed up. I wanted to scream, "Deal!" But instead, I tried waiting them out. Neither of them moved. Neither of them spoke. Keith's hands stayed on my thighs. One more minute, and I was about to pop the biggest boner of my life.

"No you won't," I scoffed.

"I will. I promise I will."

Why did he think I would want that? Did he know I was gay? Did he always know? I was so turned around in my head. I was so conflicted. This could go downhill really quickly. Was I about to get beaten up in the library?

"No you won't. No way. I'll do your paper for you, and you won't do anything."

Keith was about to say something, but Blake interrupted him. Suddenly it was like he was in charge of the situation. "Oh he will. I'll make him."

I laughed again. "You'll make him? How would you make him?"

Blake put on a devilish smile that looked like pure sex. He reached up and put one hand on my shoulder. "I'll watch."

There I sat, two of the hottest stud football players holding me in a chair in the study hall. Three hands held me down. Keith's two hands on my thighs, a look of pathetic, needy sadness in his eyes. Blake with his hand holding my shoulder smiling like he was loving every second of it.

I didn't know what to say. They weren't budging. "So what's this project?"

Against my better judgment, I did Keith's project for him. Once they had left me alone in the library study room, with the assignment written out on a sheet of paper, and a huge boner in my pre-cum soaked underwear, I went back to my dorm room and started working on his project. It was depressingly easy really. I couldn't understand how Keith would not have been able to just do it himself. I guess he really was that dumb.

I dropped his completed project off in his mailbox back at his dorm, and I didn't think anything else about it. I assumed he handed it in to his professor. I knew he'd pass with it. It was good work if I do say so myself. And that Saturday he was on the field as the starting quarterback. Blake as it turns out was a wide receiver. Between them they turned out three touchdown passes, and the team crushed their state rivals. I figured I'd never hear from Keith again.

It was about ten o'clock that night. The game had everyone on campus celebrating. Most everyone was out on the town, and the dorm was super quiet. My roommate had gone home for the weekend, so I was enjoying the peace and quiet. I was lying on my bed reading a book when I heard the knock at my door. I opened it and there standing in my doorway were Blake and Keith in their letterman jackets. Blake was smiling so wide it looked like his face was about to burst open. Keith looked like a lost puppy. Before I could say anything, Blake shoved him into my room. From the force of Blake's muscular push, Keith stumbled three or four feet into the middle of my room where he got his footing and turned to look back at me. Blake stood next to me. He closed my door and locked it. He put his big arm around my shoulder. From his height he towered over me. My head was practically under his arm. I felt tiny as fuck. Blake pulled me into his side and said, "It's time for someone to pay up." I looked up at him, and he beamed down at me with his big toothy grin.

I looked over at Blake. He looked right into my eyes with a look that landed somewhere between worried and resigned. He shrugged his shoulders and buried his hands in the pockets of his jeans. Blake barked at him. "Tell him."

Keith's eyes never left mine. "I got an A on my project."

I didn't know what to do. I had no idea how this was going to play out. "Of course you did," I said.

Blake removed his arm from my shoulder and went to the corner of my room where I had a cushioned chair. He collapsed into it, slouched back, put his hands up on each armrest. He spread his legs wide and still with that giant grin on his face said, "And now it's time to pay up."

I gasped audibly, all the air left my lungs. "Keith, what the fuck, you don't have to..."

But Blake interrupted me, "Oh the fuck he doesn't. A deal is a deal. Now put on my show."

I looked over at Blake. I looked over at Keith. My high school bully. The big meathead who tormented me. Those big black eyes staring right through me.

He took a step toward me and then another. He loomed over me, looking down at me. This big six-foot-two, beefcake football player towering over five-foot-five me. He didn't say a word. He just leaned down and planted his lips on mine and started kissing me. His hands came out of his pockets and wrapped around me. His tongue parted my lips and slid in to find mine. I gasped, and with that breath, every memory of Keith bloomed inside of me. My entire body felt like it bloomed wide open in his embrace, in his wet kiss. And I kissed him back.

I reached up and put my arms around his shoulders. I put both hands on the back of his thick meaty neck and pulled him down. If this were just some kind of practical joke, at least I was going to enjoy it until it blew up in my face. But Keith didn't pause. He just kept kissing me. And as it went on, his hand on my back went lower. He pressed it into the small of my back, and I felt his cock rub into me. He was hard. I could feel my cock at full mast in my own pants. It brushed against his, and he stopped kissing me, stopped breathing. He pulled away and looked deeply into my eyes with a slight look of surprise. His hand came around the front, and he put it over my jeans and felt my cock. He traced its length from the base as it hung to the left and kept going inch by inch under the waistband of my underwear. "Mother fucker," he said. "Billy?"

I just smiled. You see, I may be only five-five, but what I lack in height I make up for in... well, cock. It's long and it's fat. The very, very few guys who've seen it have all had this same reaction. Keith looked over at Blake who was grinning like the devil. I looked over. Blake was rubbing his own crotch watching us.

Keith looked back to me. "So you are gay, aren't you?"

Really? At this point, he now asks. "Uh, yeah."

"I always knew it," he admitted. He fell silent. His hand was still on my cock. All I could think is, dude, it seems like I'm not the only one. He stumbled on his words as he asked me, "So you want to suck my cock?"

Figures. Dumb jock. He was the one who came sheepishly into my room, dragged by his buddy. I'm the one who did his project for him. I decided enough was enough. This is the time things changed between Keith and me. I decided it was my turn to take charge. "Well, Keith. Seems like you're the one who has to pay up here. So I don't think I should be the one doing the sucking."

He tried to hide it. I could tell. He tried to keep the facade up. But as soon as I said that, I saw his eyes widen. His lips turned up in a smile. And his hand pressed just a little bit more tightly on my bulge. Blake laughed in his chair where he watched and listened. I heard as he unzipped his jeans over there in my chair. "Oh, this is getting good. I'm gonna enjoy this show."

We both looked over where the blond stud football player, opened up his jeans and yanked them down to his ankles. He pulled out an impressive cock of his own and started tugging on it. That giant grin on his face again, he called over to us, "Don't let me stop you. It's showtime."

I stepped away from Keith, breaking the contact of his hand on my bulge. I walked over to stand next to my bed and peeled off my shirt. My tiny little body appeared. I'm small, but like I said, I have a flat stomach with a nice set of abs. I kicked off my sneaks and sat down on the edge of my bed. Keith watched the whole time, and once I was sitting shirtless, I pointed to the floor at my feet. As he started to kneel down, I stopped him and decided he needed a little instruction. "Oh not yet, boy. Strip. Everything off piece by piece. Give me a show."

Keith the bully was gone, replaced by Keith the do-what-I-say football jock standing in front of me. He didn't say a word in protest. First his letterman's jacket dropped to the floor, then his hands reached down and peeled the t-shirt away from his torso and over his chest. If I have my little ridge of abs, Keith was a muscle god. There wasn't an ounce of fat on him, but his muscles bulged out. His chest was absolutely huge, wide pics covered in a light fur that trailed down over his stomach.

Then he kicked off his own sneakers and tossed them with his feet one after the other to land in a pile with mine. He bent over and pulled off his socks, then the part I was waiting for, he unsnapped his button fly jeans, pulled them apart, and dropped them. He had on a white jockstrap. Bent over, he pulled the jeans off leg by leg and threw them at Blake who put them on the floor by his chair. Blake said, "You get these back when you finish your job, dude."

I looked him over. He was such a fucking stud. No one who looked at this muscled god of a college football player would ever believe he was about to go down on cock. I have to admit he was hot as fuck in that jockstrap, but it had to go. "I said everything off," I reminded him, nodding my head toward his crotch.

He put his thumbs into the jock and paused. Looking over at Blake, then to me, he pulled it down. His cock was already rock hard and it popped out with a bounce. He threw the jock at Blake, too, who held it up to his face and sniffed it in. I was shocked by that. Blake was clearly comfortable with this. I wondered if he was gay, maybe just bi, but definitely not totally straight.

I looked back to Keith again. Standing there totally naked, while Blake and I were still fully clothed, I have to say, it was hot as fuck. He stood there completely vulnerable and couldn't look me in the eyes. I nodded to my lower body and commanded him. "Now mine." He kneeled in front of me and reached up. He undid my jeans, rolled the zipper down, and I leaned back so he could pull them off of me.

My briefs were already spotted wet with pre-cum. My cock was in full bloom underneath stretching out to the side all the way to my hip bone.

He pulled the underwear off of me, and as soon as my big cock bounced up, his mouth was on it without a second to lose. He slurped it in. The head disappeared into his mouth, and he started to move his tongue over it. He lowered down on it, bit by bit. He got halfway down and stopped. He came back up for air. I gave him a loud tsk-tsk and said, "Oh you can do better than that."

He went back down on my cock all the way to the halfway spot he'd stopped at before. Pushing down on it, I felt his throat open a little more, and he got most of my cock down his warm, wet throat.

"Fuck, man," Blake blurted out. I looked at him sitting in the corner jerking off. He'd taken off all his own clothes, too, and was jerking off his big stick.

I put my hand on Keith's head and rubbed that short, fuzzy hair. I pushed him down on my cock and directed him, "Now get to work."

I never would have guessed how Keith would look worshipping my big cock, but he moaned and slurped, and bobbed up and down on it like he'd been waiting for it all these years. I just stared down at him and watched and enjoyed. I looked over at Blake and made eye contact with him. He was loving it. These dudes, I thought, are definitely gay. They both are way too comfortable with this.

Keith started snotting up. His eyes were watering. But he didn't stop deep-throating me as far as he could. His spit was dribbling down to my balls, and I was in heaven. But I wanted more.

I looked over at Blake and said, "The deal was he would have sex with me."

Blake looked confused. "Yeah?"

I said, "Oral doesn't count."

Keith stopped sucking me. Blake looked like he was about to blow his load. I looked down at Keith. I was gonna be the bully now. "Get on the bed. On your hands and knees."

I stood up and went over to my desk drawer and found the lube I used to jerk off. When I turned back, Keith was getting on the bed. "Face your boy over there," I commanded him. This was suddenly coming naturally to me. Maybe I was the bully now. He was on his hands and knees looking over at Blake who didn't stop jerking off the whole time.

I walked behind Keith. His big, beautiful, muscular bubble butt was in the air for me on my bed. I could not believe this was happening. He was doing what I say for a change, and it was everything I always wanted. I smeared half the tube on my cock, cuz I knew it was going to take a lot of lubrication. I got up behind him and pointed the soaked head of my cock against his little butthole. I wondered if anyone had ever been in there before me.

I pushed and pushed. He moaned like he was worried, and finally after a few tries, the head of my cock popped into my high school bully. He looked over his shoulder and right into my eyes and smiled. Then he moaned my name, "Oh, Billy." He put his head down and kept moaning as I tried to push further in. He started breathing out heavy. I paused and took my time. I wanted this to last.

I ordered him, "Squeeze down on me." I felt his ass pulse on me. As soon as I did, I pushed in more. He kept moaning and grunting and breathing heavily through his teeth. I had a new idea.

I nodded over to Blake whose eyes were so wide I thought they were going to pop out of his head. "Blake," I said. "Come over here." I reached up and got my hand under Keith's chin. I could barely reach he was such a big guy, but when he felt my hand on the front of his neck, he did what I wanted and raised his head up. He moaned again, way too loud for the thin walls of my dorm, and this time I could hear it was more arousal than discomfort.

I looked at Blake and commanded him, too. "Shut him up." Blake knew exactly what I meant and put his cock in front of Keith's face. Keith immediately went down on his football buddy's big cock. And I slid the rest of my big, fat cock up his ass. He moaned with cock shoved down his throat and up his ass at the same time.

I started pushing in and out of his huge, round ass. Blake took my lead and started pumping in and out of his face. My high school bully was on his hands and knees on my dorm room bed getting spit-roasted by two big cocks. His ass completely relaxed, and I was pumping hard into him. Blake was looking right into my eyes, smiling and moaning.

We kept it up for a while until I saw Blake closing his eyes more and more. I could tell he was getting close. I looked at him and said, "Pull it out. I want you to shoot all over his face. Do it. Come for me."

Blake jerked off while holding Keith's face up in front of his cock until he clenched his teeth and blasted a stream of cum point blank at my bully. His hair caught some of it, some splashed across his forehead, and the last few blasts hit square on his half-parted lips. Blake shot stream after stream all over Keith's face. It was more than I could handle, and my cock pulsed and blasted inside him. Keith, my high school bully, my tormenter, was taking my load. I fucked Keith Taylor. The thought of it so strong in my mind, I thought I would never stop shooting. But finally the last tremors went through my body, and I pulled out.

Keith rolled over. He was still rock hard, dripping in pre-cum. He reached for his cock, but I grabbed his hand. "Oh no, no, no."

He looked at me. Blake looked at me. "You don't get to cum, buddy. You were here to pay your debt. It's done now."

Blake looked at me and let out the most evil laugh I'd ever heard. "Oh, I like the way you think."

I was the bully now. I grabbed Keith's jockstrap and rubbed it all over his cum-soaked hair. I wiped my cock with it. And I ordered him to put it on. They were wet with cum and lube, and his cock was still rock hard. Blake threw his jeans at him. I knew Keith was feeling used and powerless but fully cocked, the way I always felt in high school.

Both of them finally dressed, Keith turned to me. He put his arms around me and planted his lips on mine again. He kissed me deeply. Blake slapped him on the back of the head and said, "Now what do you say?"

Keith looked at me and said, "Thank you."

I just smiled and rubbed his still-hard cock through his jeans. Blake turned him toward the door, and he walked to it, unlocked it, and stepped out.

Blake paused there and looked at me for a moment. I was standing in the middle of my room, still naked, my cock still half hard and wet. Keith now out in the hallway, Blake stuttered, "So I have to write a research paper for my sociology class. I was wondering if you could help me out."

I smiled widely and looked at the blond hunk standing before me. "Sure, Blake, but my price has doubled."

He looked confused staring back at me. Damn, these jocks were really that stupid. I smiled as I looked him right in the eyes. "You I'm gonna fuck twice."

As he turned and stepped out of my dorm room, he smiled and said, "Deal."

Slut Conversion

By A. Bennet

I forget when exactly Luke told me he was gay. I just nodded and said, "Oh." It didn't bother me if my freshman roommate was gay. I didn't think of it again until we were at a party a few days later, and we realized he was checking out guys, and I was checking out girls, and we started commenting to the other what we thought. And we realized that each of us was pretty bad at guessing who might interest the other.

Of course like a lot of freshmen, our primary goal that first week was to learn our way around campus, drink, and fuck. And we did both a lot.

The next week after one party, I had turned in after striking out at a keg party and jerking off when I got back. I woke not long after when a very drunk Luke unlocked the door, and he and some guy stumbled onto his bed and started making out. They were trying not to be loud, which since they were drunk, meant they were extra loud, and the moonlight coming through the window let me watch as the two made out and stripped each other naked before the guy maneuvered Luke to begin sucking what looked like a very large cock. After some 69ing and some time spent licking and prepping Luke's ass, the guy rode him doggy style on the bed.

My brain thought, just pretend to be asleep, and though I was tired, my eyes were wide open. Even though I'd jerked off not long before, I was as hard as I'd ever been.

I'd never seen gay sex before that night. I'd seen countless guys' butts thrusting in and out and moaning on video, but a live sex show like this was something I'd never witnessed. It wasn't just the sound, which was raw and intense. I wished I could have jerked off watching them, because even though I wasn't touching myself, I was afraid I'd start cumming from the sight and the sound of them.

Eventually the two stopped sometime before dawn, and I think I managed to get some sleep, though I spent Sunday in an exhausted daze, leaving with my bag to go to the bathroom and then the dining hall and then the library. I couldn't quite explain why. Part of it was embarrassment. I didn't want to be in the room when the two crawled out from under the covers naked. If this were a one-night stand, I didn't want to be there for the awkward recriminations. If they were still in the mood when they got up, they could fuck without worrying about me. And if it was more than just doing the nasty, well, I could meet the guy in more clothed circumstances. It was easier to go.

I did stop in the bathroom to jerk off. Which took an embarrassingly short period of time.

The dorm was all male, and because it was so early, I managed to find a rare moment when the hall bathroom was empty. When I came out of the stall, Derek, my neighbor across the hall, was smiling at me. He didn't say a word, just smirked to let me know that he knew what I'd been up to.

At least I'm pretty sure he was grinning. The sophomore was walking from the sinks to the showers, and Derek was one of those guys who threw a towel over his shoulder and walked down the hall naked. If I had looked like him, I would have been naked all the time, too. Over six feet tall, flat stomach, with a muscular swimmers build. He had short dark hair, pierced ears and nipples, and a tuft of dark public hair. He looked like a statue of the ideal male body.

Oh yeah, and he had a massive cock that hung practically to his knees. Even flaccid it was as big as mine when I was hard.

How could anyone not stare?

It was really hard to look him in the face and be sure he was smirking.

"Struck out last night," he asked, not cruelly, gesturing at the stall.

"Yeah," I admitted.

"Happens to the best of us, man. And you're a frosh, so you'll get a better feel for where to go and who to target. You'll do okay."

"Thanks." I still wasn't sure he knew who I was.

"Derek, are you coming?"

We both turned. One of the showers was running and a slender blonde pulled the curtain back to show that he was hard and ready. It was my RA, Greg, and with him a heavyset hairy redhead who I knew I'd seen around.

"Come on in, Derek, the water's fine," the redhead called under the spray as the two played with each other. My eyes bugged out. The two were about the same size as me – and small compared to Derek. I'd seen plenty of guys in showers after gym class or in the locker room over the years, but this was different.

In high school locker rooms, you were not supposed to look. Never supposed to look. Maintain eye contact. Look at people's heads. Never look down. Never look around. If you did, people might notice. And they might say something. And maybe one person would jokingly call you something, or maybe less kindly. Maybe it would happen once and be forgotten, or maybe it would follow you. And if it followed you, the locker room might not be safe for you. So it was best to be paranoid.

College was so different.

In the locker rooms in the gym and here, everyone walked around naked and didn't care. Hell, in the quiet periods I'd heard that guys would jerk off in the showers or even fuck. It was rude to fuck with a lot of people around, I guess? It was just something that happened, and no one acted shocked.

But a threesome in the shower like this. Hell, I'd been a virgin until last week, and now I could feel my heart pounding out of my chest to the point where I felt like it must have been obvious. Or maybe not. Between the fact that my face was probably beet red and my cock was hard and uncomfortably angled in my briefs, it was a wonder I had any blood left for the rest of my body to function.

It wasn't even that the two guys were hot. It was one thing for Derek to walk through the halls naked and show off his body. I mean he looked, well, like that! And I stared just like everybody else. Looking back, I stared a lot harder than some people. But there was something so much hotter about the other two guys being naked and showing off and not caring who saw them and playing with each other like that, because they were just average looking guys. Greg was thin, and the redhead was heavy, and I was somewhere in between. We were all average sized and average looking. They had hair sprouting from their shoulders and on their butts, and they didn't look perfect, but they looked so hot.

I didn't have to be in perfect shape to be a slut and a manwhore. I just had to want it and go for it. Fuck modesty. Be greedy. Enjoy it.

If there were more blood going to my brain, I would have thought that in the moment.

Of course none of the three guys were looking at me. Greg and the redhead were playing with each other, but they were looking at Derek whose thick white cock began to bob and jerk into its full upright position. He gave it a few tugs and was looking at them and grinning.

"Duty calls," he said.

Derek didn't bother to close the curtains but put his arms around the waists of each and pulled them under the spray with him as the three made out, their hands roaming their bodies. Like it was the most natural thing in the world.

I left to avoid jerking off again, and after having breakfast with some random people, I got a lot more coffee and went to the library to study. I was very productive in the library. When I wasn't thinking about cock. Or about fucking. Or completely distracted by all the blood flowing to my own cock and not my brain.

Eventually I needed the bathroom, and I knew there were bathrooms on the third floor, but they felt hidden. A large library with multiple additions over the years sounds romantic, but it's a lot less so when you need a bathroom and they're hidden in odd corners.

When I found them, I was practically bursting from so much coffee, and it wasn't until I released a long stream and started to relax that I realized there were other people in the small bathroom with me.

Three urinals hung next to each other and to the right of them three stalls. As I washed my hands and glanced at the mirror, I could see under the dividers that two men in the end stalls were turned, facing the center one with their pants around their ankles while the guy in the center stall was kneeling on the floor. And now that I was actually paying attention to my surroundings and no longer distracted by my desperate bladder, I realized the bathroom didn't smell like urine. It smelled like cum.

My mouth went dry, and I practically ran out of the room. I didn't run far, though, and leaned against the stacks partially hidden but with a view of the bathroom door if I looked through the gaps between the books and the shelves.

Two women emerged from the women's room nearby. There was something about the way that they were walking and hanging on each other that made me think they had been doing the same things in there that the guys had been doing in the men's room. No. That was crazy. I just had sex on my mind. If I had seen the women walk out talking like this yesterday, I would have thought they were just friends. They always go the bathroom together. But maybe they were more than friends. And then I watched as three guys walked out of the bathroom separately over the course of a minute or two, each waiting until the other had gone before exiting himself, and I realized that I knew one of them from class. We had even entered the library at roughly the same time and said hello on the steps.

I was sweating. And I was hard. I wasn't sure if I was nervous or horny or maybe all of the above. It felt as though I was surrounded by sex. I wasn't getting any, but it was everywhere.

Which made the fact that I wasn't getting any feel mean and personal. Like I'd done something wrong. Of course my problem was that I wasn't doing anything right. But at the time, all I could think about was my cock.

Which was pretty common on campus it seemed.

After dinner while we were both studying at our desks, Luke said, "I hope I didn't wake you when I came in last night." I don't know what my face looked like, but clearly I shouldn't play poker.

"Sorry," he apologized. "Did we keep you awake the whole time?"

"I mean, I enjoyed it," I said, trying to say something to fill the silence. And accidentally saying more than I had intended.

"Oh? Are you–bi? I don't know. I didn't mean to assume."

"Yeah," I said. Saying it out loud for the first time. "I mean I haven't—like, I don't really have much experience. At all."

"We all start somewhere," Luke said with a shrug. "I mean if you really enjoyed it last night, and you were awake, you could have joined in."

"I thought threesome was a second date?" We both laughed and went back to working on our laptops.

I thought that was it. That maybe the next time we were out together, Luke might steer me toward someone, or we'd check out guys together. Instead, a few hours later there was a knock at the door and a guy walked in and leaned over to kiss Luke. And then Luke introduced me to Tim.

"Nice to meet you," he said. "Sorry we woke you up last night."

I stopped breathing and turned beet red. I saw he was wearing sweat pants with nothing underneath, because I could see the outline of his cock.

"Didn't mean to embarrass you, man." He leaned against my desk, and sitting in my chair, I was practically staring at his crotch. Tim didn't even try to hide that he was playing with himself through his pants, and I was hypnotized as his cock started to harden.

Luke walked over, and I stood up from my chair as he and Tim led me to Luke's bed. They sat on either side of me. They each had a hand on my leg, and Tim pulled me by the hair toward him, and we started making out. My head was swimming like I was drunk.

Tim pulled away and physically turned my head. Luke pulled me towards him by the neck, and we started making out. God, he could kiss. By the time I came up for air, Tim had his shirt off. I helped Luke take off his and the two pulled mine over my head. Tim stood in front of me and was smiling. At least I think he was smiling. His cock was straining to escape, and he had his thumbs tucked into the waistband of his sweats.

"Do you want me to take these off?"

"Yes," I said. "Please."

I felt Luke's hands on my leg and on my back, and he leaned into me. His bare chest against my shoulder, his hot breath on my ear. "Tell him what you want."

"You," I said. "Your cocks."

I hadn't gotten much more than a glimpse last night, a silhouette in moonlight, but in the flesh, it was a thick white monster, cut with a big reddish tip. Tim was a hairy guy, which I didn't care much about one way or the other. He was about as hairy as I was, compared with Luke who was hairless except for his head. I felt drunk as I reached out to hold Tim's beautiful cock and felt it grow in my hand as he stepped forward and ran his hand through my hair.

I held it by the case and licked my lips, wrapping them around the tip of his cock and running my tongue around it a few times. I don't know what I expected, but it tasted like skin. Which was such an obvious and stupid thing to think. What else would it taste like? But

Tim and Luke gave me instructions and suggestions as I played with his balls and enjoyed the feel of the tip in my mouth and tried – and failed – to fit it all down my mouth.

"Don't worry," Tim said. "This isn't a porn, and I'm not trying to fuck your face. Just enjoy the taste. Lick it. Play with it."

It was so natural in my mouth. I was a natural cocksucker. But it was more than that. More than enjoying everything, it just felt right. That musky sweat smell. That way of being both gentle and rough. It all felt so perfect.

Tim pulled me off, and Luke took over sucking, and while I played with Tim's balls, I watched what Luke did. When Tim was on the verge of cumming, I let Luke take the lead, and we sat next to each other, mouths open, looking up at Tim, who came all over our faces before the three of us made out and cleaned each other up.

"You turn," Tim said, pushing me back onto the bed. Luke began to suck my cock while Tim shoved a pillow under my butt and began licking my asshole. "I know it's a shock the first time, but relax. There are a lot of nerve endings around your anus. You have no idea how much fun this can be."

I didn't, and as both of them licked and fingered my asshole, and I'm sure my eyes rolled into the back of my head a few times before they finished. I gave Luke a facial and licked my own cum off him. After which Luke told Tim, "I want it now."

I had watched last night but not really. Now I was on the bed as Luke got on all fours and Tim lubed up his asshole and sunk that cock balls deep into Luke. There was no hesitation or tentativeness like when they were playing with me. They rutted like two animals in heat, and it was incredible to watch.

After they finished, Tim's hand was on my naked thigh. "So do you want to? Or do you want to call it a night?"

I reached out for Tim and kissed him. "Fuck me."

Tim just smiled, and he took his time lubing me up, while Luke lay next to me, making out and playing with my nipples. When Tim was ready, he kept me on my back and pulled me by my ankles to the edge of the bed in just the right position. I was smiling as he did this. It was comical. Tim leaned in and kissed me. "Are you ready?" I nodded and grinned.

They'd both fingered and licked me, but the feeling of his cock entering me hurt. There's no other word for it, even as every nerve in my body felt like it was on fire with pleasure and I felt filled.

Well, I thought I was filled. Then Tim pushed the rest of that long cock into me, and it was uncomfortable at first, but by the time he said he was going to cum soon, I knew I needed to get fucked a lot.

Tim pulled out of my ass and dangled his hard cock in front of my face. I reached out and swallowed him, tasting my ass on his cock as he pumped load after delicious load into my mouth. I couldn't swallow it all, and I must have looked a mess with his cum all over my mouth and face.

"Mmmm yummy," I said.

I actually said. "Yummy." Like a dumb whore in a porno. Well, I guess that's what I was. When confronted with a threesome, or two guys, or big cocks, I guess I turn into a total whore. And it felt so good. Even though I'd fucked three girls over the first week of school, I thought of this as losing my virginity.

After Tim left, Luke and I talked about what to do next. We were roommates who had just hooked up.

"Dating your roommate is asking for it," Luke said.

"Yeah, we shouldn't go there."

"Though there are other things we can do."

"I mean, no point in us just jerking off if the other is here."

"And maybe we should have another threesome?"

"Do you mean with Tim? Or just in general?" I asked.

"Both," Luke said. "Now let's 69, slut."

"I am a slut, aren't I?" I said with a laugh as he climbed on top of me.

After that I went out every night, and between hanging out at the bar in the basement of the student center, evening events at the LGBTQ center, working out and cruising the locker room afterwards, or just going to the library to "study" in that bathroom, I was fucking, getting fucked, sucking off, and fooling around with people of any gender at least once a night. I was up for anything, and people were more than happy to deliver. I realized that it just took a little effort, a little work. No tricks or bullshit. From experienced older students who were more than happy to teach me, to other frosh coming into their own and willing to experiment in every way, I found a lot of ways to get to know other students and have fun together.

On Fridays I slept in because I didn't have classes until the afternoon, so I decided to walk naked down the hall from my room to the bathroom in only flip flops and a towel thrown over my shoulder. I loved the feel of the breeze on my cock and balls. And as I walked past his room, Derek's door opened.

I turned, and he was standing there, towel over his shoulder and flip flops on his feet. I don't think I looked bad dressed, or rather undressed, like that. But I didn't look like a gorgeous man with a porn star size cock. I didn't even pretend not to stare. I just hoped I was drooling.

"Hey."

"Hey."

"Nice weather."

He was alone, and I could feel my cock growing. He had that effect on me. Derek noticed and grinned.

"So are you, um, taking a shower," I asked. Yes, I asked that standing in the hallway, with both of us naked with our cocks hanging out. Well, he was hanging. I was hard as a rock. Are you taking a shower. I'm just that smart. God, it was a wonder I wasn't a virgin being this dumb. Derek didn't say anything, just reached out and stroked my hard cock. He smelled of sweat and last night's vodka, and he didn't say a word—just held my cock and led my down the hall like that toward the bathroom. "We could, you know, shower together. To conserve water," I suggested, talking to fill the silence and to keep from cumming too soon as he pushed the bathroom open and tugged me inside.

He smiled. "Water conservation is important," he said. "And conserving water with bisexual manwhores is always fun. Did you know that every bi dude on campus is a total slut?"

"No," I said. "But this is only my first month of college."

Derek laughed and, holding onto my cock, led me into the shower stall. Yes, I was a total slut because of water conservation. "Well slut, the bathroom tends to be empty very early, late at night or late morning. Which makes them the best times for us to shower in groups." I nodded, and he pushed me against the wall, and we made out.

"Have you ever had shower sex, " he asked. I shook my head, and he got a big grin. "Well, I'm happy to show you. But first why don't you show me what you've learned so far." If I didn't pick up the hint, he put his hands on my shoulders, and I dropped down and held onto his ass as I sucked his cock until he came down my throat.

He told me not to swallow, and we shared his delicious load, and then he returned the favor. I didn't last long. It took just seconds before I unloaded down his throat.

"Sorry," I apologized. He stood and fed me my own cum.

"You're fine," he said. "You'll last longer next time. And we'll just have to keep doing this so you can get some stamina."

Derek dropped to his knees and between his tongue in my ass and his hands on my cock and balls, he made me spray on the shower wall. I had no idea a tongue could feel that good. A week ago I had no idea my asshole could give me so much pleasure.

He maneuvered me to lean against the wall with both hands and got behind me, the shower spraying onto my back and his chest. Lubing my hole, he went slow, but I leaned my head into the spray to help muffle my moans as his thick tool inched deeper and deeper into me. It started feeling tight and uncomfortable, but then I began to feel full as Derek began fucking me. His hand on my hips, I wasn't sure if he was slamming into me or if he was pulling me on and off his cock. It was probably a little bit of both.

Moaning into my ear, he said, "I'm going to cum inside you." I just moaned and fucked back onto his cock harder. As I felt him unload into my hole, all I could think was that I was on the right track to being a good slut.

It's true what they say. You really can discover yourself at college.

The Adjunct

by Matthew Cooper

I had no one to blame but myself. Being a liberal arts major, I avoided my science core requirements. There I was second semester, senior year, ready to graduate in May, and I realized I still needed three credits in science. Most of my friends got those out of the way in freshman and sophomore years. Then when all I could think about was graduation and getting on with my life, I had to face one more class that I was dreading.

I'm not stupid. No, really, I'm not. It's just that I care more for art and acting than I do chemicals and dissecting frogs. So I put it off and pretended it would just go away. It had been two years since my friends were trudging through the course catalog looking for something to take that would fulfill the requirement without being too difficult.

We had all sorts of nicknames for the classes preferred by our fellow liberal arts majors. It was rumored that Geology was a pretty simple science class, so we dubbed it Rocks for Jocks. Every student athlete who thought he had a chance at turning pro took that one. The frat boys all thought Astronomy was an easy one. Thus we called it Stars for Studs. Jocks, frat boys, I thought this can't be that bad. Maybe I'll luck out and have some lowerclassman eye candy while I pained my way through a class I couldn't give two shits about.

There I was nearing the end of the fall semester of senior year when what I should have been worrying about was a senior independent study project and sending out resumes, and I was stuck looking through the course catalog for a 101 entry-level course. And it didn't look good. Only one section of Geology was being offered, and it was at the horrendous time of 8 AM. Fuck no. Monday-Wednesday-Friday.

I didn't know which sounded worse. Monday or Friday. That wasn't happening.

My finger zig-zagged down the list of classes and section. Fuck. Astronomy wasn't being offered at all. What was I going to do. I definitely was not going to delay my graduation and take something the following summer or fall. No. I was through. I wanted to get on with life along with all my friends who were making plans for apartments and moves into the city. No way I was going to still be on this fucking campus after May.

I decided it was worth a visit to my faculty adviser, Professor Thompson. Honestly, in three and a half years, I hadn't met with him since the day we were introduced in freshman year. He knew me, of course. He was a professor in the English department, and I had taken a few classes with him, but I never scheduled any appointments to talk about me and my coursework or anything like that.

He had a surprised look on his face when I appeared at his door during his office hours.

"Matty," he said. "To what do I owe this pleasure?"

I sat in his side chair next to his desk. "Well, I need to fulfill my last core requirement, and I'm having a hard time finding a class."

"Core requirement? Students usually blow through those in freshman and sophomore years. Why have you put it off?"

I just shrugged and said simply, "Science."

He leaned back in his chair and nodded, "Oh I see. What are the options?"

"That's the thing. There doesn't seem to be any."

"No Astronomy? No Geology? That's what you kids seem to prefer."

I put the course catalog down on his desk opened to the start of the science department's offerings. "Well, there's one section of Geology."

"And?"

I was embarrassed of my laziness but hoped he would understand. "It's 8 o'clock in the morning."

Professor Thompson let out a big sigh. "Well, a senior certainly needs his sleep, doesn't he?" I'm sure he was mocking me. "But it's only what," he looked at the booklet. "Three days a week."

I just looked him in the eyes. He looked back at me. He understood.

"Well," he said. "I'm your adviser to help you with your major and keep you on track with what you should take, but that's really more about your major. I really can't do anything about core requirements. It's not even in my school let alone my department. I guess if you want to get this done by May, you're going to have to take something."

We just stared at each other for a few more minutes until he picked up the booklet and started reading over the list of dreadful classes. He rolled his eyes a few times and made a few grunting sounds. I knew as an English professor he must understand what a nightmare this was going to be. I'd rather be reading Dickens than studying fruit flies or whatever it was they did in the sciences.

He leaned forward and pointed down at the tiny print. "Well, you could always go with one of the intro courses. How about Intro to Biology? Since you're not, shall we say, a morning person, here's an evening class. And it's only once a week."

I was very familiar with those classes. Rather than meet three times a week for an hour, they were once a week, but you were imprisoned for three hours, from 5 until 8. Professor Thompson was waiting for my reaction. I just wished he could give me a permission slip or something to waive the requirement, but I knew that wasn't a thing.

"What night of the week is it?" Please don't say Thursday or Friday. Please don't say Thursday or Friday.

"Wednesday. That shouldn't be too bad, don't you think?"

"Do you know anything about the class? Is it hard," I asked. I never said I was an eager student.

Thompson laughed and handed the booklet back to me. "I'm sure it will be full of freshmen. How hard could it be?"

As I walked out of his office, I looked down at the course listing he had circled. Next to the class, BIO101: Intro to Biology, I saw the instructor name and came to a halt in the middle of the hallway. McGuinness. The notorious Doctor McGuinness. Chair of the Biology department. He was the worst. Even biology majors avoided his classes he was so tough. Fuck my life.

The day I had been dreading for months finally arrived. First Wednesday of the first week of my last semester. I dragged my hesitant body across campus to the science building at 4:50 PM. I would have preferred to be making my way to the cafeteria for dinner or to a friend's room to hang out, but there I was heading to a building I'd avoided for four years

I found the classroom number on the wall and looked in. It was one of those mini-amphitheater style rooms. With Intro classes there were always dozens and dozens of students in every section. I heard some of them could reach 100 students or more.

There were already a lot of bodies dotting the tiered rows when I went in. Looking around I didn't recognize anyone, which made sense, being away from my department and taking a class that probably never had a senior in it. I sat alone near the top of the room as far from the professor's sunken stage area as I could get.

The room kept filling until it was about half full. There must have been well over 50 people. I scoped the faces for hotties. Not a frat boy or college jock to be seen. I looked at my watch. Class should be starting. Three hours to go. I texted a few friends before the professor came in to see if anyone was around afterward for a drink or late dinner. No one responded. How could this get any worse?

Five minutes after the class should have started, I saw people getting antsy. Ten minutes, still no professor, people started chatting, where is he, what's going on, should someone go find him. Fifteen minutes, a few people started to pack their bags and leave. One obviously over-achieving girl stood up and announced, "I'm going to the office to find out where he is."

I took my phone back out and texted my friends again. Pete texted me back, and we made plans to meet up when I got out of class. I texted, prof no show might be out early. He sent a line of emojis that included smiley faces and beers. Something to look forward to at least.

The intrepid girl came back in and seemed almost happy or relieved. "He's coming." Did she think that was good news or something?

Doctor McGuinness trudged into the room from the top and descended the wide stairs one by one. He had nothing in his hands. When he got to the lecture area, he looked flustered and dusty like a stereotypical old professor. His eyebrows were like giant, gray caterpillars on his face. His huge, red nose was pockmarked, and his clothes hung from him like he hadn't washed them in months.

He cleared his throat and announced, "Well, as you know, I was scheduled to teach this course. But unfortunately, my schedule will not accommodate that. I'm sure you're not too sad to hear that. We are still looking for a replacement, and I'm sorry to tell you that unless we find someone to teach this course by next week, we will have to cancel it. You're free to switch to another section or find another class to take in its place. The drop/add fee will be waived."

The same girl who went to find him raised her hand, "When will we know for sure?"

McGuinness shrugged. "Come back next week, and if we have a professor, we will continue with this section. If not, the drop/add period is two weeks, so you'll have time to replace this with another class. But if you'd rather just switch now, please see the department secretary, and she will sign your change forms." And with that he climbed back up to the top of the room and left.

The room erupted in complaining and whining. What the fuck were these freshmen all worried about? They had three more years. I had to get this class in now, or I was royally screwed. Still, at least I wasn't going to have to worry about ballbuster McGuinness teaching the class. I walked out and decided to wait it out until the next week. Hopefully they would get a replacement. If not, I guess it would be a semester of waking up at the asscrack of dawn three days a week.

A week later, there I was sitting in that damn amphitheater classroom again. Five minutes before class should start, and there were only about 15-20 students. I guess they all transferred out to other options. I probably should have done the same. I could not face the thought of 8 AM classes. I had spent the last three and a half years a master of planning out my week. I rarely had a class before 10. I usually was able to keep a full day free every week without any classes. I even took some summer classes in order to get more credits in so I didn't have to overburden myself during the fall and spring.

I looked around the room. A lot of worried faces just stared down at their books. Some people were doodling on notebooks. A few were texting. Eager girl from the week before was sitting up straight in her chair staring forward. I hated her already.

I looked at the clock. It was like deja vu. The class should have started five minutes ago when I heard the scrape of the door opening at the top of the room right near where I was sitting in one of the last rows. I turned and saw a head pop in the crack and look around. It was a very nice head. Messy brown hair sat atop an incredibly handsome face. He looked like he could be my age instead of a freshman. I hadn't noticed him the week before but hoped he came and sat next to me.

"Um," he called into the room. "Is this Intro to Bio?"

Eager girl, of course, was the first to answer. "Yes. Section BA."

I looked back up to the newcomer. A smile bloomed on his face showing off a set of dimples that made my heart skip a beat. I'm a sucker for dimples. I perked up in my seat and took a closer look. That messy mop of hair looked wet. Sweaty. He ducked back out, and the door closed again. I tried to will him back into the room with my mind so I could get a better look.

It must have worked, because the door opened again, and he stepped in. My eyes were immediately so wide, they could have popped out of my head. This guy was wearing a biker's suit. You know the kind, totally form-fitting, shiny, showing every curve of the body. He held a backpack in front of himself and had the textbook under his arm. He was standing on the stair right next to me hesitantly. I had to try to make him come closer. I pulled my bag away from the seat next to me and nodded at it, suggesting he sit next to me. I wanted to get a closer look at those curves, because in the first moment, I already saw an amazing rounded and sculpted chest tightly fit into the fabric of his shiny, blue bodysuit. It had a zipper front that was pulled all the way up. His biceps bulged as he gripped the backpack in one arm and kept the other tight to hold the textbook between his arm and his slim, sleek torso.

He looked at me and realized I was nodding at the empty seat next to me with a smile. He silently gave me an awkward shrug and stepped down toward the front of the room. Geez, rejected already. But at least as he stepped down, I got a glimpse from the back. You have to love bikers. The spandex suit ended just above his knees, but it was a little higher than that where my eyes were glued. His ass was round and muscular and tight and stuffed into that blue fabric like it was about to explode. So was I. That was an ass for the ages, I could tell. Now I know that kind of suit is going to make anyone look good, but that was a butt to be sculpted in marble. I felt my cock come to attention immediately.

Biker dude kept going down the steps until he made it to the front of the room. What the fuck. "Hello," he said. "I, um, I must apologize for my outfit. I just got the call a few hours ago. Anyway, I am going to be your teacher for this class. And, well, again, I do apologize for my... I'm a competitive cyclist, and I biked here. I'm training for a long-distance race, and I need all the practice I can get. Um, but any way, sorry, I'm Mr. Towson. Emile Towson. I, uh, don't usually teach here, so we can keep it casual if you want to just call me Emile."

He turned to the large desk next to him and brought his backpack up in an arc and dropped it there. Audible gasps could be heard all across the room, including mine. With the backpack out of the way, I and everyone else got a full view of the huge bulge in his skintight suit. His cock was perfectly outlined trailing to the left. I will never forget the detail of it. Resting in a fold of the blue fabric, his cock spread out horizontally above the rounded bulge of his balls. And let me tell you, it was impressive. If that was how it filled his pants soft, I wanted to see it hard.

Emile heard the gasps and looked for one instant confused, then he looked down at himself. He turned the most adorable shade of red. Even his ears flared with color. For a moment I thought he was going to puke. His hands immediately covered his junk, and he looked around the room with sheer terror in his eyes. "Um, perhaps I should... um... sit down while I teach tonight."

I was immediately filled with an overwhelming heat from my head to my toes that focused itself on my own crotch. I sat there for the next three hours just staring at him. I don't think I even opened my textbook. I bit on my pen until it was wet and bent. Even through two short ten-minute breaks Emile, or Professor Towson, or whatever I was supposed to call him, stayed planted in his chair behind that desk.

At 7:45, I think he could tell he had lost everyone's attention. "OK, well it's a few minutes early, but since this is our first class, let's wrap it up. I know you all would like to get out of here." He closed his book on the desk in front of him and waited for everyone to pack their things and make their way to the door. I had another idea. I just had to come up with some question or other to bring down to hot teacher's desk.

So I took my time picking up my backpack and pretending to put my book away and my pen. I pulled out my phone and pretended to check my messages. I realized that several of the girls in the class had already beat me to it. There were at least three girls already in the teaching area, huddling around his desk, asking him inane questions about the lesson. I mean, come on, they were so obvious. It was Chapter One. What questions could they have?

But I couldn't help myself. I joined them. Stepping down the stairs one by one, closer and closer to Professor Bulge, I couldn't think what I was going to ask him. I noticed I was the only guy still there. I think the teacher did, too, because when he looked my way, I got the distinct impression he knew these girls were all there for something other than questions about biology. They were asking about assignments and grading and midterms. I mean, really, it was the first week, well, second, and this chick is asking about the midterm?

He was answering all their questions until eager chick asked him, "So you haven't taught here before?"

He smiled charmingly, "No, I'm just acting as an adjunct. I'm a medical student myself."

"But we don't have a medical school," she said with an annoying tone of know-it-all.

"No," Emile answered here. "I go to the state university. In Newton."

I spoke up finally, "But that's like thirty miles from here."

He looked right at me. He locked eyes with me. I could tell he was hoping to get away from all the attention these freshman girls were dripping on him. "Thirty-two, actually. I know. I biked it."

Eager beat me to it, "You biked here thirty-two miles? And now you're biking back again?"

She was obviously a genius. But Emile smiled nicely, "Yes. I'm training for a long-distance race. A hundred and fifty miles. Thirty is nothing to me."

The girls were still surrounding him. I was behind two of them. Clearly I wasn't going to get to talk to him alone, but I didn't want to leave him like this either, so I just lingered there.

Finally, he put a dismissive tone into his voice, "So yes, it's late. If you'll all excuse me, I'm sure you have more fun things to do on a college campus than talk to an old professor."

That's when I realized he didn't want to stand up until we were all gone. The shorts. That bulge. He was embarrassed and hoping they would all just clear out before he had to stand up. One by one the girls were giving up. I could tell each of them wanted to be the last one there, but I wasn't going to give up no way, no how. It took like twenty minutes, and now it was later than if the class had gone to full time, but I won out. Eager beaver was the last one out the door, but that left me standing there with just my hot stud biker professor and my own already-half-hard cock.

He looked at me. I looked at him. Then I realized he was wondering what I wanted. I kinda stuttered at him. "So, I just thought I would save you. Freshman girls, you know? They can be annoying."

He let out a big sigh and looked into my eyes with relief. "Yeah, thank you. I definitely wasn't thinking when I left the house. This is really embarrassing." He nodded down at his lap that was still hidden behind the desk.

"Oh, yeah, sorry. You probably want to get out of here. Um, so you're really biking thirty-two miles home now? At night, in the dark?"

He stood up. Fuck, yes. I was wondering if he was going to finally give up on getting rid of me. And there it was right in front of me, an arm's reach away. That unbelievable bulge right there. I wanted to push him down and grab it, but I thought that might not be a good idea. I did, however, like the fact that he was now comfortable standing up.

Probably because it was just us guys now. He had no idea I was just as bad as the giggling girls.

"I do it all the time. Really, this is a shorter ride than what I typically do any way." He smiled at me as he pulled his backpack onto his shoulder and nodded his chin toward the stairs up to the door, obviously suggesting we make our way out.

On our way up the stairs, I tried to let him go first so I could get another look at that meaty ass again, too, but he gestured his hand toward the stairs and said, "Please."

"So, I'm looking forward to the class. I put off taking a science class for too long. I'm just relieved this one didn't get canceled."

"Oh, you're not a science major then?"

"Oh, no. I'm... I'm an English major. This is just a core requirement class. We have to take science, and well, I graduate in May, and this is my last chance to get it in."

As we reached the top of the classroom, I hesitated with my last few words. I took a few seconds too long to reach for the door handle, and we both ended up grabbing it at the same time. His hand landed on mine on the handle. I didn't move a muscle. I left it there sandwiched on the handle under his. For what felt a millisecond too long, he didn't release his grip. I looked back into his eyes. He stuttered, "Oh sorry. Let me get that." He took his hand from mine, then waited for me to let go of the handle, and he opened the door.

In the hallway, I turned to him and couldn't think of what I could say that would get him to agree to come back to my apartment and let me strip him naked and suck his cock and fuck his round, meaty ass. So I just said, "Well, good night. See you next week."

He smiled at me, and at that moment, we both turned toward a booming voice down the hall. "Mister Towson, a word?" It was Doctor McGuinness standing in his office door.

Emile looked at me, his eyes wide. "I think I may be in trouble."

In a moment of idiocy, I spoke without thinking. "It's probably cuz of your bulge."

Emile glared back at me, shocked. His mouth was wide open, and I could tell he skipped a breath. "Whaaa...." It was my turn to flush a vibrant red. I could tell he wanted to crawl under a rock. He was as embarrassed as I was about what I had said, maybe more so. "I maybe should have changed."

"Well," I said as I turned away. "Good night, and... good luck?"

For a week I thought of nothing else but Emile Towson's ass. And Emile Towson's bulge. I wondered how big his cock was. I wondered if he was cut or uncut. I wondered if he was gay. Yeah, I didn't even know that, so what use was it obsessing over him? And even if he were, he was my professor.

I went from dreading having to take a science class to desperately waiting for Wednesday nights to get here. I would get to spend three hours eye-fucking my teacher. That next Wednesday, I was even twenty minutes early to class. And I sat a lot closer to the front of the room. Third row. I'm not a total stalker.

I did notice that the girls in the class had thrown sweatpants aside and were now all dressed up like they were going out to a club or dinner. Eager beaver looked like she put on make-up for the first time ever. Someone was going to have to explain color palate to her, though. There were several mini-skirts, and the whole room smelled like a department store perfume counter.

Finally a few minutes before the start of class, the door scraped open against the floor, and Emile bounded down the stairs to stand in front of us all. Damn. He wore a smart pair of beige khakis and a button-down shirt. His hair was combed back. I'm not going to lie. He looked smoking hot. But I did prefer the giant bulge in the bike suit from the previous week.

As he put his backpack down and pulled out his textbook and erased the board, I got a closer glimpse. His shirt had the first two or three buttons undone, and sure enough, underneath I got a quick flash of that bright royal blue. He was still wearing his sheer, form-fitting suit underneath.

Again for three hours I tried to concentrate, and Emile was a great lecturer. I was understanding the material, and for a while I even cared. But my mind kept wandering to ripping his clothes off. As the three hours wore on, whatever he had put in his hair to slick it back started wearing off a little, and a few wispy strands came loose and fell over his forehead. It made him even hotter. He looked like the perfect, nerdy professor trying to hide the fact that he was actually a smoking hot stud. I'd seen enough porn to know it turned me on like crazy.

Class ended, and again, Emile was surrounded by the girls of the class. Each of them came up with the most idiotic questions to ask that really were so unnecessary. I'm sure he saw right through them, but he was nothing but gracious and addressed all their made-up concerns. I stayed in my seat.

As each girl asked her question, Emile would answer it then look over at me. His look was half, why are you still here and half gratitude. At least I hoped. When the last of the gaggle finally asked her third question, he answered her but added, "Is there anything else I can help you with?"

She got the hint and walked to the door, but she turned to look at me with a glare first. What, did she think I was trying to cock-block her? Because I was. When she finally huffed through the door, I turned my head back to Emile who was staring at me. "So, did you get in trouble last week?"

He smiled and laughed, "You know, I thought you would ask. Turns out, no. He didn't even notice, or at least didn't say anything. He just needed me to fill out a few forms to get paid."

"Well, that's good," I said with far too much finality. I didn't want to end the conversation. I was hoping he wouldn't just walk out.

"You did though."

I stared at him and didn't know what to say.

But he didn't leave me hanging there and added, "Notice, that is. And for that I apologize. It was definitely completely unprofessional of me to dress like that, and since you, shall we say, brought it up, I wanted to apologize."

"Oh, you don't owe me an apology. I didn't mind…" Fuck. Me and my big mouth again. "I mean, not that I didn't mind, I mean, like, not that it bothered me, I mean.." I just trailed off while beating myself up inside.

Emile just smiled at me. "So we can both agree that's the past."

Fuck no. I want it to happen again. I want you to dress like that again. I want to see your bulge and your ass again. "Sure. In the past."

"Well, if you don't have any questions for me, I'll be off."

"Sure." How could I get him to stay? "See you next week. Um, be careful out there." And I gave him a thumbs up.

He smiled back at me as he bounded up the stairs and out of the room. A fucking thumbs up? What the fuck.

I don't think I'd ever been so tongue-tied around a guy before. I was typically smooth as shit. In three years I had quite the reputation with my buddies for being able to score some questioning hottie or barely-out sophomore. I think I'd fucked the entire gay-straight alliance on campus and not just the gay ones.

This was different though. A professor. An older guy. I felt off my game. Like I couldn't control what would happen. Even though I was convinced it was nothing. Nothing was going to happen. But I couldn't stop thinking about him. I was definitely obsessing. Turned out, I didn't have to wait that long.

It was the first week of February, and all the news reports were calling for a significant blizzard on Thursday morning. Everyone was excited at the prospect of a huge storm, canceled classes, snowball fights on the quad. Nothing beat a snowstorm on campus.

As I walked over to the science building, I realized that in all the chatter and anticipation of the storm, I finally stopped obsessing over Professor Hottie. For once, my entire Wednesday afternoon had not been spent in a daze thinking about him. But as I got to the other side of campus, a light snow had begun to fall.

By the time I was walking into the building, it was coming down steady. Sitting myself into my third row seat that had become my usual spot, everyone was buzzing about tomorrow's classes most likely being canceled when Emile came in. Snow painted his smooth, brown hair. His cheeks were rosy, and when he smiled, and those dimples came out along with the pinkish hue, I popped a boner in seconds. God, fuck, he was hot. Dimples, rosy cheeks, he was cute hot, if you know what I mean. I started obsessing about him again.

I could not stop eye-fucking him through the entire class. The snow made his hair more disheveled than usual. The red color in his cheeks faded mostly. But his ass in those khakis, I could not stop staring every time he turned to use the blackboard. I was perving out hard. Maybe it was the excitement of the snowstorm and everyone being in such a buzzing good mood. But every now and then I got a tiny glimpse of that tight biker suit under his smart and polished exterior.

Each break I went to the outside door to check on the snow. It was just a dusting after the first hour of class, but after two hours, it was already a few inches deep. I was hoping Emile would let us go early. But he kept teaching and before I knew it, it was 8 PM. The girls didn't linger to hit on him like they usually did. He was busily packing his bag. Students were booking for the door. I was still staring at him.

He smiled at me. "Did you go outside at the break," he asked.

"Yeah."

"And how is it?"

He looked at me with concern. "It was already a few inches deep an hour ago," I told him.

"Fuck."

I opened my eyes wide. Of course, I hear that every day, but it was somehow different coming from a professor. He realized, "I'm sorry. I'm sorry. I shouldn't curse."

I shrugged for him with a smile, "No biggie. What's up?"

He looked right into my eyes. It was like he'd lost his puppy or something. "I knew I shouldn't have biked here tonight. I thought it wasn't going to snow until tomorrow."

"Oh fuck is right. You can't bike in this," I said seriously concerned for him.

"I know. I guess I could call a cab. But fuck, sorry, I... even if I could get one in the storm, I have no idea how much that would cost."

I was suddenly aware of the hard-on growing in my pants.

"You think there's an affordable hotel nearby?"

I almost choked I blurted the words out so fast. "You can stay at my place!"

Emile bowed his head and shrugged. He was shaking his head back and forth. "Matthew, thank you. I couldn't do that. And besides, a professor is not allowed in the dorms."

"But I don't live in the dorms. I have an apartment off campus."

He looked at me. I realized that might make a difference. I could push this. But then he said, "Still, that's very nice of you to offer. But it's definitely inappropriate."

I was finding my inner control. I felt every fiber of my mind locking on target. "Emile," I said.

He looked at me. It was the first time I'd used his first name. He didn't say anything.

"You told us to call you Emile."

I waited a moment, but he didn't say anything.

"Come on. You're stuck. You can't bike thirty miles in a snowstorm. I've had professors at my place before. We've had English department get-togethers, and professors came. My adviser came to my last party." I was lying.

He looked at me. "I don't know."

I stood up and walked down to stand next to him. "It's no big deal. I'm glad I can help you out."

He looked right into my eyes. I hoped he couldn't see what I wanted to happen, or maybe I did want him to. I didn't know if I would even be able to try. He was just so fucking hot, I couldn't not try. "Fine," he said.

Yes. Fuck. Yes. I was as hard as a rock standing there in front of him. It was my turn to put my backpack in front of myself. "Cool. Well, let's go."

Professor Hottie was sitting on my couch. Lots of deep breathing and focus on the walk over to my apartment calmed my raging hard-on. Now I had to somehow get him out of his clothes and onto my cock. I knew it wasn't going to be easy, no matter how much I was hoping he wanted it as much as I did.

"You want a beer," I offered. That would be a good start.

"Are you twenty-one," he asked with a smile.

"Yes. I told you. I'm a senior."

"OK."

I went to the kitchen but kept an eye on him. Even the back of his head with his smooth, snow-wet hair was turning me on. I saw him glancing around the room. There wasn't really much to see. I had the couch and a coffee table, a television on a cheap stand with a gaming system on the floor in front of it. The coatrack near the door now had two wet jackets on it—his and mine hanging there together.

Other than a dinette set in the kitchen and my bedroom furniture in the other room, I was the typical poor college student. He probably had a beautiful apartment that looked right out of a high-end furniture store. Maybe some day.

I came around the couch. "Sorry, I don't have much."

He smiled up at me as he took the cheap beer from my hand. "Oh, I know what it's like. I'm still in school myself, and trust me, you don't want to know what my student loans are like."

"So you're a student, too, then. See we're not so different." I'm such a dork. "So how old are you? If you don't mind my asking."

He snickered. "Twenty-seven."

"That's only six years older than me. Most professors are ancient."

"Glad you don't consider me that way."

He looked uncomfortable. I was hoping he wasn't regretting coming over. I had to get him more relaxed, but I didn't want beer to do the work. "You're still in your teacher clothes. I'm going to change into some sweats. Why don't you make yourself comfortable?" Make yourself comfortable? What was I, in some shitty romance movie?

I got up and went into my bedroom. I made a point not to close the door. I saw Emile stand up and unbutton his shirt. Yes. Pulling open my dresser, I picked out a pair of grey sweats. Sitting on my bed, I peeled off my jeans and tossed them on the floor. Then thinking about it, I pulled off my underwear, too. I don't want to brag, but Professor Hottie isn't the only one that hangs low even soft. I pulled the sweats on and checked myself in the mirror. Yeah, it was obvious. With a few yanks and another look out to my living room where he was taking off his khakis and sitting back down in just that form-fitting biker suit, I added a little bit more life to my cock. I threw on a ratty old t-shirt that was pretty much threadbare, and I was ready.

Walking back across the living room to the couch, I got a look at his face. He was smiling until he turned to look at me. Maybe I did a little bit too good of a job fluffing myself up, because his eyes trailed down from my face and right to my swinging cock free inside my loose sweats. In that split second, it was make or break. He tried to cover up having looked and pulled his eyes back up to my face. He was still smiling as a wash of that adorable blush bloomed in his cheeks.

Sitting next to him, I had to try my hardest not to touch the blue fabric that had a tight grip on his body. It was my turn to look him up and down. Damn, I could see the contour of his muscles over every inch of him. His chest, his tight stomach. That's when I realized he was holding his beer can in his crotch, trying to hide that bulge I knew was there.

I sat on my knee so I was facing him. I purposely sat close on the couch. "Are you comfortable in your biking gear? I could loan you some sweats or something."

"Oh," he said. "That's OK. I, well, maybe to sleep in. But I don't have, you know, anything with me." I just smiled and didn't say anything. I wasn't letting him off the hook that easily. I tilted my head like I didn't understand. "You know, I don't even have any underwear."

"Right. Well, you've been in that suit all day. Maybe we should get you out of it."

He turned his head to look at me. I think he was feeling super awkward now. I had to slow-roll this, or I was going to lose him. Besides, I realized at this point, he's probably not even gay. What was I thinking? This was stupid. If this went south, it was going to be a very uncomfortable evening with him stuck here in my apartment.

But he was still looking over at me. He still hadn't spoken. I raised one eyebrow and stared right into his eyes. I shifted my weight a little and spread my leg out a little wider. He broke the stare first and turned his head forward and lifted his beer to take a swig. I did the same but kept looking at him.

As he dropped the beer can down from his mouth, he bent his head down slightly, and then I saw it. His eyes turned back to me for an instant but not at my face. He looked at my sweats, right at my junk. For one quick second, they lingered. I had him on the hook.

Swallowing his beer, he finally answered, "Yeah, I should probably change. If you have another pair of sweats or something."

"Sure."

I stood up, and he did, too. We stood facing each other. We were only inches apart—I made sure of that. I was going to have to go into the bedroom and get him something to change into, but instead I just stood there looking at him. I realized in that moment that I was a good three or so inches taller than he was. I loved the way his head had to tilt a little to look me in the eyes.

"Really," he said meekly. "I don't know how I can thank you enough for this. You have to let me repay you in some way."

"Well," I paused. Do I dare? It was all or nothing. I wanted this so bad. I put it all on the line. "You could let me fuck you."

He opened his lips, but no sound came out for a moment. He also didn't break away or go tearing for the door or punch me, though, so that was a good sign. His mouth fell open in utter shock. "Matthew, I..." He trailed off.

After what I had just said, I didn't know what I could possibly do to recover from this if he was offended. But what would he do? Would he flee out into the night in the middle of snowstorm? I had nothing left to say. All I could do was wait for his reaction.

"I, um..." He was still looking at me, so that was another good sign. "I've never... um, I'm not..." I smiled and resigned myself to the failure.

"You're straight."

"Well, yeah. I mean, no. Not entirely, I just... I've never..."

Ok, that wasn't a hard no. And he still hadn't punched me or slapped me or fled. "You've never had sex with a man?"

"Well, no."

I had to press on. "But you want to."

He sighed out, a full breath escaped through his lips. He stuttered, "But.. you're my student."

I smiled. "You're an adjunct. And I'm just taking the class 'cuz I have to." If I didn't keep going, this was going to come to a crashing halt. I reached my hand up and took the zipper of his suit between my two fingers and pulled down really, really slowly, exposing a few more inches of his chest. That beautiful chest with its firm rounded shape came into view a little more. It was so incredibly smooth, not a hair to be seen.

He didn't stop me. He just kept looking me in the eyes. The zipper kept going down. Now it was reaching over his stomach. His tight little stomach, first one row of abs, then another. Fuck this dude was in such great shape.

He breathed in and out again. If he didn't stop me soon, my hand on his zipper was about to reach his belly button and even lower. His lips hung open. His hands still didn't move to stop me. Finally he whispered, "No one can know."

Bam. Fuck. Yes. We have a go. This was going to happen. He was mine. I finished with that zipper to the very bottom until a bit of his cock appeared. It was still trailing inside the suit, reaching far to the left. Damn, it was long. And now I could tell it was almost fully hard. I reached in and pulled it out. Fuck, yeah, it was huge. And on a guy so much shorter than me, it looked like a monster.

I looked back up into his eyes. They were wide now. I flashed a dirty smile at him full of desire. "I'll never tell," I said and planted my lips on his mouth. He moaned deeply into my mouth. I pushed my tongue between his lips, and he finally moved his arms, lifting them up and draping them over my shoulders. His head tilted back, and his mouth opened wider inviting my tongue in to explore.

I wrapped my arms around him and took those two thick round orbs of his ass into both of my hands. Oh I have wanted to touch him for so long. I held onto them as I kissed him deeper than I'd ever kissed anyone before. He clasped his hands behind my neck, and we stood there locked together and kissing for a long while.

My hands explored him, and I was desperate to get him out of that suit, no matter how hot he looked in it. I pulled it down his shoulders. He had to take his hands away from me as I pried his body free from the tight blue suit. It slid down exposing his torso inch by inch until it was resting on his hips. I paused a moment and looked at him. Fuck, his body was insane. Tight muscles from neck to hips, thick shoulders and arms, that chest so perfect, a six pack of abs. That insanely huge cock bobbing out in front of him. He even had those lines on his hips that pointed in a V right at it. My hands were all over him as he just stared at me.

I pushed the suit down his legs, and he stepped out of it. I tossed it over the back of the couch. There he was. Professor Hottie standing in my living room. Naked. I could feel the power you have over someone when they are completely naked, and you're still fully clothed. Fuck, I loved it. The tables of professor/student authority were completely flipped. The fact I was so much younger didn't matter. I was in charge, and he was mine.

This time he came back into me and wrapped his arms back around me and kissed me deeply. This time his tongue came for my lips and into my mouth. I sucked it firmly, and he moaned again. The sound of it was so hot, like he was ready to let me do whatever I wanted to him.

I put my hands back on the orbs of his now bare ass. Oh fuck it was smooth. I traced the lines of the two mounds, the crest across his lower back, then my fingers found the crack and slid up and down into it. I bent myself down a little and reached lower and planted a finger right on his puckered hole. He pulled back a little and breathed out with a huge gasp.

I tickled him finger after finger. I could feel his cock as hard as a rock against my stomach. I stopped kissing him and looked right into his eyes as I pushed a finger against his tight, dry hole. I could only get in up to the first knuckle, not even an inch. That was going to change by the end of the night.

"Nobody's ever..," he sighed.

I pulled my finger away. "Well, that's about to change." I took his hand in mine and put it on my cock. He instantly closed a grip around it and slid it up and down. I sensed he was measuring it in his hand. I nodded my head. He continued to feel my cock through my sweats. His eyes were as wide as I'd ever seen them. His mouth hung open. "Yeah, you're gonna take all of it. Aren't you?"

"Yes," he moaned. It's all he said. I took his hand away from my cock, and taking it in mine, I led him to my bedroom.

I pushed him down on my bed, and he fell across the middle of it. I stood at the end between his feet and pulled off my t-shirt. He looked up at me and stared at my torso. I wasn't a muscled god like him, but I was twenty-one, and I worked out, I'm sure he liked what he saw. His eyes were wide. It was probably the first time he was lying on a bed naked looking up at a man, and I could tell he was loving it.

I reached down and pushed on the top of my sweats. They were loose and dropped straight to the floor after they were freed from my rock-hard cock. It bounced up and pointed straight at Emile. He stared at it, a hunger in his eyes. "That's so big," he said.

"Not as big as yours."

"Almost." He lifted himself up and reached out his hand to grab it. His fingers curled around it. "And thick."

I smiled at him "Don't worry. I'll go slow. We have all night."

He kept sliding his hand up and down on my cock. His head was just inches away, and I knew what I wanted as an appetizer. I reached my hand out and rested it lightly on the back of his head. I urged him forward, and he knew what to do. He opened his mouth and took the head of my cock in. I don't have to tell you. The warmth and the wetness were incredible, but hotter was the thought that he was doing this for the very first time.

He slid down on it, testing himself. He went halfway, then all the way back up so just the head rested between his lips. For a beginner he was already good at keeping his teeth clear. He went back down, a little further this time. Good boy. Good professor.

Up and down, my cock slid in and out of his mouth. More and more spit soaked each time, it shined until it dripped. He had his eyes closed, and I watched him sucking my cock. But I had a bigger plan. I put my hand on the side of his face and urged him back. He let my cock slide out and looked up at me, spit soaking his lips and dripping down his chin.

I leaned down and kissed him and tasted my own cock on his lips. I pushed him back on the bed and walked over to my nightstand. In the drawer, I found what I needed. Grabbing a condom and a tube of lube, I went back to the end of the bed with them in hand. I looked down at him. His cock was dripping with pre-cum. "Roll over," I said. "On your stomach."

He obeyed in silence. Fuck, Professor Hottie was turning out to be very obedient. "Spread your legs for me." He did. "Stick your ass up for me. Show it to me." He put more of his weight onto his knees, and tilted his hips. His big, round, muscular ass was up in the air for me. His entire body was smooth and hairless except his legs, which had a small amount of brown fuzz on them. Fuck this was hot. I felt like just standing there and taking in the beauty of it.

But I couldn't help myself. I had to have more. I squeezed the lube out in my hand, slicked up a finger, and started tickling his tiny, little puckered hole. I pushed on it with each sliding touch. I pushed a little harder, and it let me in. I circled that finger around slowly, spreading the lube and pushing further and further in. Emile moaned and held his head down.

I slid my finger in and out of him. He was breathing fast and making little sounds. I pushed a second finger together with the other, and pried him open a little more. "Oh fuck," he called out. "Oh, Matthew."

"You can take it," I assured him. "That's my boy. Squeeze." He did, and I felt the pressure on my two fingers tighten then relax. He let me in a little more. I twisted and prodded. He squeezed and moaned. "That's it. You're so tight. Relax for me. That's it."

He started rocking his hips. I knew he was loving it. My fingers were pushing in and out of him now. I pulled them out and added even more lube and pushed them back in. His ass opened for them right away.

"Are you ready for this cock?"

He let out a long, slow moan on his breath, "Ohhhhhhhhhh...." Then he said what I had wanted to hear from him for weeks now. "Fuck me," he moaned.

I didn't waste another minute. I tore that condom wrapper open, slid it onto my impossibly hard cock, and kneeled closer in between his legs. He spread them out further and pushed his ass in the air a little more. I smeared even more lube on my cock until it was dripping, then put it in place right on his slick hole.

Leaning over him, I pushed. His hole was still tight. Not to brag, but two fingers are a lot smaller than my cock. I pushed. Emile moaned and breathed out. I pushed a little more, and finally the head of my cock was inside my professor. I stayed there for a minute or so. He kept his head down, still breathing loudly. Then I felt him push his hips back. He was pushing back on my cock, letting in another inch of it.

Oh, fuck, he wanted this. My dirty little teacher was about to get his first fuck ever. I felt like I had conquered the world. I got the exact thing that I had wanted. I couldn't believe it was happening, and I was going to take everything I wanted. I pushed slowly and steadily until my full cock was planted in his ass. I lowered myself on top of him and wrapped my arms around that amazing, muscled torso.

I brushed my tongue across his ear and sucked the lobe. I was planted all the way deep inside his ass, but I still added a little more pressure. "Take it," I whispered in his ear. "Good boy."

He tilted his head toward my face. He looked me in the eyes over his shoulder. "Fuck me," he begged.

I could feel the round orbs of his ass pressed against my hips. I slowly slid my cock out of him and pushed it back into him again all the way deep. I reached one arm around and planted it across his stomach, one finger pressing on his belly button. I pushed up on it, and his ass rose to meet my thrusts. I pushed my other arm around his upper torso and searched that smooth, rounded chest until I found a nipple and squeezed. "Oh fuck. Oh fuck," he cried out.

His ass was so relaxed now. I could not believe how much he'd opened up for me, first time and all. It was soaked with lube, and I wanted it more than anything. I started sliding in and out of him, faster and faster, pushing at the end as hard as I could. I wanted his ass so badly, I was piston fucking him like crazy. He was bouncing on my mattress and moaning and whimpering and taking it like a champ.

I wasn't going to last, and I couldn't help it. With one final thrust, I cried out and felt my cock pulse. I came loud and hard and dropped down onto his back. He just lay there underneath me not moving. I put my hand on his hand above his head, and he interlocked his fingers with mine. We lay there like that for a long time until I reached down and held the end of my cock and let it slide out of him.

Rolling off of him, I laid down next to him. He stayed there on his stomach and looked over at me. He had a huge grin on his face. "That was amazing," he whispered to me.

"You're so beautiful."

He rolled onto his side to face me. I looked up and down his body. He was still hard. I reached over and put my hand around it. He leaned in and kissed me hard and passionately. I let go of his cock and wrapped my arms around him. I pulled him on top of me, and he let his legs fall on each side of my body and squeezed my hips with his thighs.

"You haven't come yet," I said.

"No," he answered.

Emile kissed me on the mouth. His cock was still so hard and pushing into me, after more kissing and forcing my tongue into his mouth, he made my cock come to life again. He pulled up and looked at me. I stared at him and had an idea. He could tell. "What," he asked me.

"I'm going to fuck you again."

And I did.

About the Contributors

A. Bennet is a lifelong New Englander who majored in history and minored in French, smoking pot, and un-learning modesty. He's a bisexual slut trying to make up for the fact that his college career wasn't nearly as much fun as his story suggests. This is his first published short story.

Brady P. Books has been a bartender, massage therapist, art school model, bank teller, school janitor, librarian, tutor, and teacher. With a last name like Books, he has been convinced since childhood that he would one day be a bestselling author.

Matthew Cooper is an editor and writer of erotica and erotic romance. He is the editor of the anthology Surprising Myself for Insatiable Press and has been a guest speaker and panelist at several writing conferences. Originally from New Jersey, he has lived in Manhattan, San Francisco, and now lives in Wilton Manors, Florida. You can connect with him online at www.facebook.com/authormatthewcooper.

Eric Del Carlo's erotica has appeared for decades in anthologies from Cleis Press, Circlet Press, and other publishing houses. He is also a much-published mainstream science fiction writer.

Michael Roberts has been a devotee of gay sex for years. He has published stories about

it in leading gay magazines, in cumpilations from Cleis Press, Alyson Books, and

STARbooks Press, as well as in a literary—not a literal—appearance on

cruisingforsex.com.

WRITE FOR US!

Coming soon, with a little bit of luck, FRAT BOYS AND DORM ROOMS 2: More Gay, Erotic Stories from the Best Four Years of Your Life. Yeah, we definitely have to work on that subtitle. Do you have a story set at college? Submit to us for consideration, and your story could be shared with horny men everywhere. See below for our email address.

Looking for a publisher? Wilton Springs Press focuses on new voices and new writers. Our focuses include gay fiction, erotica, romance, and more. For more information, contact us at wiltonspringspress@gmail.com.

www.ingramcontent.com/pod-product-compliance
Lightning Source LLC
Chambersburg PA
CBHW061300120726
48001CB00001B/392